I0619578

MASON & HALL SERIES

BOOK TWO

STRANGER
DNA

Gippy Adams Henry

J.J. Legacy Publishing
Runnemede, N.J.

Graphic Design Artist for *Stranger DNA* Cover@2021: Joe Savin
Fine Artist for *Stranger DNA* Cover Painting @2021: Judy Adams Jones
Stranger DNA—Mason & Hall Series/Book Two

Author: Gippy Adams Henry
ISBN-13-978-0-578-92341-3

DEDICATION

In Memory of my Loving Son
Elwood Chuck Pacewicz

An amazing father to two daughters:
Samantha Pacewicz & Brittanie Pacewicz
&
A wonderful brother to two sisters:
Loralee A. Cardie & Angela M. Pacewicz
&
A loving Pop to four Grandchildren

ACKNOWLEDGEMENTS

With love and gratitude, I would like to thank Judy Adams Jones, the fine artist who put her heart and soul into painting the amazing work-of-art in the center of this cover. In time, the reader will understand just what the scene stands for in the Stranger DNA story.

With love and appreciation, I once again get to enjoy my Graphic Designer, Joe Savin's expertise in developing the unusual and eye-catching set-up of the surrounding cover. His ability to reveal the terror along with the beauty is one among many of his great gifts.

I am grateful for the time and work the Developmental and Substantial Editor: Danny DeCillis has brought to this story with his constructive critique. With a PhD in literature and 18 years as a professional writer and editor for a policy research institute, his knowledge in the field is priceless.

To My Readers,

Thank You for your support

I hope my responses in book two
address the foreshadowing completely
from book one and please you.

But never think that is the end.

CHAPTER ONE

Michael Pearson finally arrived at the only place that brought him peace. He turned into the circle driveway and parked his car in front of their house, as he had done for over fourteen years. Getting out of the car and tossing his keys onto the driver's seat, he headed to the back of his 6.3 acres of ground. It surrounded the sphere-shaped silver and gray stone glass house. When he reached the very end of his property, he lit a cigarette and sat on the edge of a tall shiny new gravestone. The light breeze around his property felt good.

"Well, Bro, I did everything I could to keep you straight and out of trouble since I found you a few decades ago. I even went to prison for you, setting things up to look like I murdered those people. But you still had to go after Dana's family and get yourself killed." Michael rose and paced, avoiding the still soft dirt that was delivered the day before to fill the open grave for his brother.

He turned back. "I forgot to mention that Britt McKenzie survived the car incident. If it weren't for her, I would still be behind bars."

As he turned to put another cigarette out in a tall metal container nearby, he could hear the engine of a vehicle coming around his driveway. He quickly walked back toward the house. By the time he got there, to his surprise, Britt McKenzie was leaning on the front doorbell.

"Hi. Did you come to see Matthew's gravestone?"

When she faced him, he couldn't believe how run down and tired she appeared. Her eyes were red and swollen, and she had a tissue to her nose. As she spoke, her movements were jumpy. "I forgot you had him transferred. Could we do that another time?" Her eyes filled with tears. "I came by to cry on your shoulder before I end my life."

Michael's eyebrows raised as he realized this was more serious than he thought. "That's a bit dramatic, Britt. What's going on?"

He led her around the house to the side glass patio and pulled out a chair for her. He took her coat and put it around another chair, "Get it all out or I won't be able to help you."

She coughed a few times, then she raised her head up. "I've been seeing a married man for a few months. Please don't judge me."

"I haven't spoken a word yet. Go on."

She had a tissue to her eyes. "Without warning, he ended it. He told me he would never leave his wife."

He tried to steer her in the right direction, "Your plans to go to college in September will be a new beginning. Moving into the condominium in Philadelphia was a good move. Plus, you have the entire top apartment to yourself. Are you happy there?"

"Sure. Meg's a sweetheart, and she barely charges me any rent. I can't complain and I thank you for getting me the apartment. What good is it, though, without someone to love me? This man is the one I dreamed about. He is nothing like Matthew—the horrible way he treated me."

"This guy has a huge drawback . . . he's married. You are so much better than this, my friend. Give it time. You will grieve, but he is doing you a favor by giving you your life back. I am sorry you got into this mess. But this break-up would have happened at some other time in the future."

"How can you say that when I'm crushed?" She dabbed at her tears. "I thought you would be the one person who would understand."

Michael's heart went out to her, but he knew he had to be the strong one. "I feel terrible for you. Yet nothing you do will bring this guy back. Most men do not leave their wife for another woman. You should concentrate on your future. You are going to study nursing. One day, you may become a doctor and live a great life. Changes happen because there is light and joy around the corner. That's where you are supposed to be—not with a married man who will always put you last."

Britt suddenly stood. "I know you are right. Thanks for listening. You have always been the strong one in both mine and Matthew's life." She pushed the patio door open and took a deep breath.

Michael walked Britt to her car with his arm around her shoulder. She kissed him on the cheek.

There was a lot of rustling in the trees. Yet, there was no wind. The property was dense like a forest around the grounds. They could not see who or what caused all the thrashing of the branches off the trees.

"It's probably deer running through," he assured her. He closed her car door and waved as she drove away around the circle to the road.

Walking back to the patio door, he locked up and turned toward his car just as his phone buzzed in his pocket. "Hello."

"It's Britt. I thought you should know that when I reached the road, I spotted Ben getting into someone's car at the end of the tree line. They took off right as I was going to pull out. I almost ran into them."

At first, Michael didn't take her seriously. "There's no way it was my son. He knows nothing about this property."

"He does now. The few times the Campanella's had us over during the holidays, it gave me the opportunity to meet your family, including Ben. I remember his face. He looked straight at mine as they drove past my car."

Michael could not respond for a second. His throat seemed to dry up. He struggled to compose himself, coughing a few times to cover up the shock that his son found his secret location. He wondered just how much Ben knew. He doubted his son was aware of his fiancé, Nicky, and their daughter Michaela. He wiped the sweat from his clammy hands, thankful they were not home at this time.

"Thanks for the heads-up. I will talk to him as soon as possible."

Michael got into his car and drove out onto the road, with Ben on his mind. *He tried to put together an explanation of how he had this house in Bucks County. What would he say to his son?* Suddenly, pulling over to the side of the road he felt a rage come up inside his chest, and he slammed the dashboard with his fist. *He loved Ben and never wanted to make him feel he wasn't important to him.* He took a deep breath and cried out, "What have we done to our son, Jessica?" *He lived with her knowing she was seeing his best friend for years after they married. When he found someone to love, he felt it was okay . . . he needed love too. But look at the damage to his child.*

CHAPTER TWO

Philadelphia, PA

That afternoon, Michael pulled into his funeral home lot and grabbed his briefcase. It held the documents he planned to share with his wife, Jessica. He had finally decided to confront her with his plans, which would begin today. Tired of the charades in their marriage and Ben's constant outbursts, bad behavior, skipping school, not coming home for days, and drugs; this is not where he wanted his son to be at sixteen-years-old. He even had to get Ben out of jail a few months ago for robbing a gas station for drug money.

After taking a deep breath, he got out of his car and walked to their apartment entrance next door to their funeral home, unlocked the door and entered. Jessica sat in the nook in the kitchen and was sipping hot coffee. Michael sat across from her.

"I'll get you coffee," she stood.

He took her hand. "That can wait. I need you to sit and listen to what I have to say."

She sat back in her chair at the table.

Michael opened his briefcase and took out the paperwork. He then looked over at her. "It's time for us to go our separate ways. Our pretense of living a happy life is over. I don't think we have fooled our children or made them more comfortable because we stayed together all these years. We sleep in different rooms, barely speak to one another unless there is a problem in the house, and we pretend to be a happy family at dinner time and when we have friends over. That is not the life I want to live in the future or have my children continue to suffer through. It's all a lie."

Jessica's face turned pale as she coughed more than a few times.

Michael stood and touched her shoulder. "Are you okay?"

"I suddenly became nauseous. You never indicated you were this unhappy. Is it my extra weight?"

He went back to his chair. "You must think I'm a fool who believes you are not still sleeping with my ex-friend for over fourteen years! Might I remind you that we were only intimate for the two births of our children, Becky and Ben in all the years I lived here with you."

His wife didn't deny it. She put her head down for a second. There were no tears when she looked up. He felt she knew in her heart that it had to be over now.

"Here's the process I laid out." He spread the legal documents out on the table. "I need you to sign these divorce papers. Take your time and read them over. The funeral home is in our names and will stay that way. You and the children can live here for as long as you wish. You will note the alimony total you will receive once a month is listed on there. If you have a problem with that number, we can discuss it. You should get your own lawyer to look it over. I'm hoping we won't have to take this to court."

Michael waited while she glanced over the papers.

"What about the furniture and other décor should I choose to move to another location with the children.

"You can keep it all. My only desire is that everything involving the funeral home business continues. I will hire someone to take over the finances. I think that is best. Most importantly, I want joint custody of our children . . . at least Ben. My plan for Becky will always be to take over this business when I retire one day. Please do not take that away from her."

"I would never interfere in the business or hurt Becky that way. You should know me better than that."

Michael stared at her for a moment. "Most of the time, I don't think I know you at all."

"I'm sorry you feel that way. I'll contact a lawyer and have him look over all your requests. Where will you live?"

"I would rather not discuss that with you until I speak with Becky. In fact, do you have any idea where our son is today?"

"I would hope he's in school."

"Probably not. But don't worry. I'll find him."

"Is he in trouble again?"

"Not that I have heard, but I would like to have a chat with him."

Jessica stood. "Could I get one last hug?"

He felt the wetness of her cheek. Then he turned away and left the apartment. Once he reached his car, he left out a sigh of relief before starting the engine.

CHAPTER THREE

Philadelphia, PA

As soon as Michael left Jessica, he drove to Meg Carson's condominium in the center of the city. He was relieved when no one tailed him this time. For once he felt free on the road, unlike his recent trips where he has been followed by a stalker.

When he arrived in the city, he kept his eyes open wide, always searching for his son. He knew Ben had not been in school for a week.

When he pulled into Meg's street, full of condominiums on both sides, he parked his car, got out and rang the doorbell. She greeted him with her usual cheerful smile. *Meg was always someone he could confide in, and she knew he would be there for her. They had been friends for a long time. In fact, she had been married to his brother. She was also kind enough recently to rent the top floor in her condo to their mutual friend, Britt McKenzie.*

"Do you mind if I make a few calls before we chat?" he asked as she held the door open for him.

"Go ahead. I'll make a fresh pot of coffee. Take your time."

He spent twenty-five minutes calling all of Ben's friends. No one acknowledged they saw his son at any time that week. When he made his last contact to his best friend's mother, she hadn't seen his son lately. She knew Josh was supposed to drive him somewhere later today.

He gave up and went into the living room to sit next to Meg. She handed him a mug of hot coffee. "Thanks." He began to sip it slowly, drawing in the aroma.

"What's happening or can't you say?"

"I'm looking for Ben. No one has seen him since he took off from school a week ago. It terrifies me to think what that boy could be up to these days. After a few sips of coffee, he stood up, stretched, and paced for a few minutes. "Enough about us. How are you, Meg?"

"I can't complain. It's nice having Britt upstairs. We have a good time together when we go to the nail salon or have dinner down here. Yet, she seems upset lately. Have you spoken with her recently?"

"She's dealing with something big. I'm sure she will share it with you soon. I think she needs someone to lean on like you, to help her get over the issue and move on."

"I would be happy to come to her aid in any way I can."

"I always like spending time with you. I think I know you well enough to guess that you have a problem you are struggling with also. I heard it in your voice over the phone yesterday."

"Guilty." Meg's smile was contagious even in serious conversations. "It's pretty deep and requires a decision soon. Once I sort it in my mind, I'll share it with you. I know I can trust you not to pass it on to others until I'm ready."

"Of course. Now, I'm off to check on Britt if that's okay?"

"Since when do you have to ask? Take your coffee with you." She rose from the sofa and headed for the kitchen. "Let me fill a thermos for her." She handed it to him before he made a left turn outside the door and took the two flights of stairs up to Britt's apartment on the third floor. The second floor was still vacant.

Juggling the two coffees, he hit the knocker using his elbow. He heard rustling around, so he knew she was awake. He waited patiently then knocked again. Britt opened the door. She looked terrible. Her hair was in disarray. She had no make-up on, which he had never witnessed before. She was barely clothed, and her eyes were red and puffy.

"Looks like I stopped by in time to save you from yourself, "Michael teased. He tried to get a smile from her. "This should wake you up." He handed her the thermos. "Compliments of your lovely neighbor and landlord. Now, talk to me," he encouraged.

They sat across from one another in her little living room. "I don't have much to say. My mind is filled with my lover, who I will never see again. I envy his wife. I think how great it would have been for me to take her place."

"It's obviously over, Britt. You might benefit by seeing someone. I have a friend in this area who is a professional counselor for women. You might like talking with her as an outsider from your circle to get her opinion on your situation."

"Sure, whatever." She barely sipped the coffee and finally sat it on the table between them.

"First, you have to promise me you will go to the appointments."

There was silence for a moment. He leaned over and touched her hand, while peering into her sad eyes.

"I promise," she finally agreed. She then stood and grabbed her robe. "Would you mind if I shower now?"

"Not at all. I should get going . . . always a lot to do. I will send you the information for the counselor later today."

"Okay, sure. You are a great friend." She left him standing at the top of the steps and headed toward the bathroom.

He shook his head, shut the door, then went downstairs to say goodbye to Meg. *Poor kid. She's been through so much in the past with my brother. The thought of what Matthew did to her for five years weighed heavily on him as he took the stairs back down to her floor.*

Back in Meg's apartment, he found her working on one of her children's books she writes, paints, and publishes. It was laid out on her desk in the den.

"How did it go?"

"She still seems depressed and not in a good place. When I left, she was going toward the bathroom for a shower. I hope that and the coffee makes her more alert, although I am doubtful."

"My day is going to get busy later, but I'll check on her before I leave here," she offered. "I'm sure you have a heavy schedule as always, Michael."

"I do. I'd better run. It was good to see you. Talk soon."

He got into his car and sat a moment to gather his thoughts. Before pulling away, he tried to get Nick

Campanella on the phone. He and Dana had been in Paris since January and were due home soon. He had to ask him a question he couldn't carry in his thoughts any longer. There was no answer.

He left a message but knew the question he had for his friend would gnaw at him while he waited for a return call.

CHAPTER FOUR

Bucks County, PA

After he left Meg and couldn't get Nick on the phone, Michael pulled out from her street with churning in his head. His thoughts were of divorcing his wife, Britt's problems, his son still missing, and the worry of telling his children about the changes in their lives. He felt a strong need to drive up to his Bucks County home instead of working at the funeral home today. It was the one place where he felt loved and comfortable. He knew his daughter Becky would be covering their business phones. There were no planned services that day.

Halfway to his home, he had to pull over to the side of the road to take a return call. "Hi Nick."

"Sorry I missed your call earlier. We are leaving in a few minutes for a special dinner in Paris. Dana finished the portrait here. Is everything okay on your end?"

"Sure, I need to run something by you."

"Okay, what's up?"

"Do you have any idea who Britt is dating?"

"No, I wasn't aware she was seeing someone. Is she okay?"

"Yes. Forget it. I was just curious. I'm on the road so I'll talk to you later. Safe trip home."

"You too, buddy."

For the rest of the drive, he put classical music on to distract him from over-thinking.

When he pulled into his driveway about an hour later, he parked in front of their house. Nicky Collins ran out to greet him. They hugged. She helped him get his work from the back of the car. *The thought of how lucky he was to have met her many years ago filled his mind. It was right after he had discovered his wife was having an affair with his best friend. They had been together for a long time too.*

Nicky studied him. "You look happy." He held the front door to their home open for her. He couldn't believe how long he had been living two lives and he was excited to surprise his true love today.

"Honey, are you okay? You seem dazed."

They put away his briefcase and other things in his study, then hugged again. This time he gave her a passionate kiss. "I have good news."

"That's wonderful. I'll pour you coffee first. Have you had lunch?"

"Coffee is fine. I would prefer talking if that's okay. Were you in the middle of grading papers?"

"No, go ahead." She placed a hot cup on the dining room table in front of him and sat waiting for him to speak.

"Today, I gave Jessica divorce papers to sign. She agreed it's time."

"Unbelievable!" With tears in her deep brown eyes, Nicky moved her petite body over and sat on his lap. "You did not tell me you were ready to do this. What prompted it?"

"I believe you will agree that we both wanted this for a long time. I am tired of living in a lifeless marriage. I miss you and Michaela when I'm not able to be here, and my son is suffering from that farce of a marriage. It's time we are all together, Nicky."

"No complaints here," she kissed him again. "I'm ecstatic." She danced around the room. He stood and lifted her up into his arms. "I feel the same way. You and our children are my life. We have been engaged way too long. Let's start planning that wedding." They could hear the front door close.

"Hi Dad!" *He loved how excited their daughter acted when she did get to see him. They had missed so many days and nights together.*

"Did you just get here?" Their beautiful fourteen-year-old, Michaela Pearson, was beaming. He could hear the excitement in her voice. It broke his heart knowing she didn't get the attention she had deserved in the past.

When she finished hanging up her coat and school-bag in a nearby closet, she pulled her thick black hair up into a ponytail and hugged her dad tightly. *He didn't ever want to let go again. He knew he could now give his youngest child a lot more attention.*

"I've only been here about an hour . . . waiting for you. Both my beautiful girls should be dressing for dinner while I take a shower. I am driving us to a fabulous restaurant to celebrate."

"What are we celebrating?" Michaela asked.

"Life, Sweetheart." The three of them walked up the wide staircase together.

CHAPTER FIVE

Philadelphia, PA

Earlier that afternoon, Ben hurried down the street to Meg's condominium and rang the top bell for Britt's apartment. *He hated that even in the cold weather his forehead broke out in sprinkles of sweat when he was angry. His heart was racing by the time she opened the front door to the building.*

He turned away, feeling someone was behind him.

"Hi, didn't mean to stare."

He glared at a middle-aged man facing him at a close distance, which was more irritation for him. "Can I help you?"

"Jim Cash." He offered his hand, but Ben ignored it. "Since you're standing here, I thought I'd say hello. Are you new to the neighborhood?"

"No. I'm visiting someone. Is that okay?" His voice was edgy.

"Certainly. Sorry I interrupted. Have a good day." Mr. Cash walked away after noticing the young woman's head peering out the door.

Ben turned to face Britt.

"It's you! What are you doing here?" She tried to slam the door on him.

He shoved the door in, causing Britt to lose her balance and fall backward. "You don't get to send me away," he yelled at her, his voice loud and his fists sticking up toward her face.

She had landed on the bottom step of the stairs that led to her third-floor apartment. When she stood, her one leg went out to kick him in the groin, but he quickly backed up. "Dam you!" she yelled. "I'm calling the police." She jumped up and ran up the stairs with Ben following. She tried to slam her door at the top, but he was too quick. He put his foot in the door to her apartment. She grabbed her phone and ran towards the bathroom but dropped it along the way. He grabbed up her phone from the floor, kicked in the bathroom door and tossed it in the toilet. She turned and sprayed him with hairspray, just missing his eyes.

He grabbed her. "Now are you going to listen? He twisted her wrist, and then pulled her by one arm and led her into the living room in the front area of the apartment. "I need some answers from you to-day. If I get them, I won't hurt you."

"Sure. I believe that from a drug addict!"

Ben's face was red now, his hands in fists by his side. "You are having an affair with my dad, aren't you? Don't lie to me."

A shocked expression spread across her face. "Of course not. Your dad and I are good friends. I've known him a long time. Does this have anything to do with you being in Bucks County the other day?"

"Yes. I finally caught the two of you!" His voice kept rising. "I want you to stay away from my dad. Get it?"

She quickly ran out through her open double glass doors to the front deck of her apartment. She screamed, "Help me!" to anyone who could hear her three floors below.

"Stop yelling." He tried to holler over her. They struggled for a while as she continued screaming. *Fortunately,* Ben thought, *the street looked empty, but the other condos across the road facing them could have people lurking from their terrace.* He finally grabbed both her arms as she pulled back toward the railing. *He didn't mean for all this to happen but couldn't control her.*

"I'll let go of you, but you must calm down first. We can sit and talk about this. I promise not to harm you."

She gave in and he led her back into the living room where they sat across from one another. Nervous now, he believed he might be wrong and offered her some Methamphetamine, which she accepted. Afterwards, she leaned down under the sofa and grabbed an open bottle of whisky.

"Yo! What are you doing?"

"Drinking. That's what I do best when I hate my life."

"Put it down. You can't mix whiskey with what I just gave you."

"Like you care. No one cares, so neither do I."

He reached over and tried to grab the bottle, but she had a tight grip on it. She jumped up and guzzled a lot more before he could get it out of her hands.

"Get out of my apartment now!" she yelled. "I'm not having an affair with your dad." She walked to the bathroom. He heard the water running and assumed she was going to relax in a bath. Afraid to leave her alone in there, he waited an hour, while getting her to respond off and on that she was okay. Then she finally came out in a robe, her long wet hair dripping. She glared at him. "Leave now!"

He felt she sounded a bit fuzzy but figured it was the whisky. Afraid to pursue it any further, he left. "She is really crazy off her rocker," he mumbled as he ran down the stairs and out the front door to his friend's car. He jumped in and breathed a sigh of relief.

His friend, Josh, who had been waiting in the car all this time, looked over at him, then his watch. "Good thing I brought a book to read. I didn't think you'd be up there this long. How'd it go?" He waited for his friend to answer before starting the car.

Ben was irritated and frustrated at this point. He was dripping of sweat and cursing. "Just drive. Get us out of here!"

CHAPTER SIX

Philadelphia, PA

Around three p.m. that same day, Meg had left her condo to have an early dinner with her daughter, Laney Carson Campanella and her son-in-law, Charlie Donato Campanella. They lived in a high-rise condominium in the city. It was only a fifteen-minute drive from her condo, especially since the traffic wasn't heavy at that time of day.

Before leaving, she had made sure Britt was okay, although she still seemed distant. She then locked up the front of the building and got into her car. As she drove down the street, she had spotted Michael's son getting out of a car a few buildings down from hers. He looked straight into her eyes then continued down the street. Meg was so distracted by the traffic at that time, seeing him in her neighborhood had slipped her mind by the time she reached her destination and greeted her family.

Once in her daughter's home, their Chocolate Lab, "Choco" was the first to greet Meg. She stooped down. "You are such a good boy," she pat him on the head.

Charlie and Laney's condo looked beautiful. Their décor was pastel used throughout the home, and her daughter made an excellent dinner and dessert.

When Meg had arrived, all the food was on the dining room table. She loved the combination of roast and browned potatoes. Laney knew they were her mom's favorite. The three of them made small talk while eating.

After dinner, she looked at her watch. It was only four p.m., so no reason to rush home. Over her favorite, fresh baked apple pie, they chatted about Charlie and Laney's progress in their first year in college. Laney was doing well in accounting, and they discussed at length Charlie's latest paintings from the art college he was attending in Philadelphia. They led her into their small gallery to view them. She was impressed with his talent. Yet the main conversation always turned to Laney's pregnancy with their first child.

"Are you feeling any better now that you are getting closer to your due date?" She touched her daughter's belly. She felt her future grandson move under her hand. They both smiled.

"I'm sure he will be a beautiful, healthy baby."

"How can you say that Mom, when you are aware that there are all kinds of possibilities that our baby might not be healthy? I wish Charlie and I had known we had the same genes before I got pregnant. Why didn't anyone in the family tell us when we first started dating?"

Meg gulped. *It was heartbreaking to witness her beautiful daughter's grief. She knew it wasn't healthy for her pregnancy. But she couldn't bring herself to explain things to Laney and risk losing her love.*

"You are both too upset. Let's pick another subject to discuss," Charlie suggested. "We can talk about this another time. I don't think anyone is guilty of what happened. It was a choice made decades ago that wasn't shared with the family. That's how we were put in this position. We weren't even part of the universe at that time. Who could have known then that the choice made at that moment by another family member, might affect us almost a century later?"

"You're right. I'm sorry, Mom."

As her daughter dabbed at her tears, it ripped Meg's heart in two. "No need, Laney. I understand your fears. As difficult as this will be, I think it's time I shared some important information with you and Charlie."

Imagining the worst reactions, Meg shook inside as she wished she hadn't offered to finally confess her secret held over many years. Her saving moment was the doorbell.

Charlie walked over to their front door on the 18th floor and hit the intercom.

"Hey, guys. It's Nephtalie and Lisa. Can we come up?"

"Sure." He pushed the button on the wall to release the front door downstairs. "You don't mind, do you Meg?"

"Of course not. In fact, I should be going." She was happy to escape, not having to tell her story to the kids.

"Please stay, Mom. You'll like Nephtalie's friend Lisa."

"Maybe for an hour or so, then I must go," She insisted. She was grateful their friend's visit avoided the conversation she'd hoped would never happen.

CHAPTER SEVEN

Philadelphia, PA

Michael was in Philadelphia to try and find his son, when he received a call from Detective Brock Mason from the Philadelphia Police Precinct.

"There's been an accident in front of Meg Carson's condominium. I need you to get over there and see what is happening. We'll be there shortly."

"What kind of accident?" he asked the detective just as the call was cut off. *He was shocked. Yes, he was an undertaker with his own funeral home, but he did not usually go out to accidents. Since the detectives had done so much for him in the past, he figured he would comply this time.*

By the time he reached Meg's street, it was five-fifteen p.m. He noted the police responders had already cleared the area and blocked the street at both ends. Leaving his car at the corner, he wondered what this accident had to do with him. He knew Meg was safe at Charlie and Laney's home. Then the horror settled into his brain—it could be Britt! He stopped in the middle of the street, trying to take a deep breath. There were numerous police officers going door-to-door. He guessed they were searching for suspects and/or witnesses if this was a homicide case.

One of the policemen came over to him and asked for his identification. Shaking inside now, he handed it over. Then he was led down the center of the street— not the pavement. They stopped in front of Meg's condo where he noted a white sheet on the ground covering a body. Every nerve in his anatomy awoke when he viewed the pool of blood on the ground. It surrounded the head area of the victim.

To calm himself, he thought about how the weather was cold that day. It was now in the thirties, which meant this incident must have happened recently. From a small part of the deceased exposed, he noted the body was not yet decomposed. As he turned away, he noticed the medical examiner's white van across the street. *His worst fears ran through his mind. He knew he was in a state of shock with his thoughts.* His legs trembled and his stomach rumbled.

Turning again, he noticed people across the street hanging over their terraces. He coughed a few times, feeling his saliva freeze in his throat. *What am I doing? He realized he was not concentrating on the scene before him but thinking about unimportant details at that moment.*

Interrupting his thoughts, a police officer came over and stood at one side of the body. The first responder on the scene spoke, "I understand from Detective Mason that you are the emergency contact for this victim."

He drew in his breath now that the deceased was confirmed in his mind. Then he grabbed his chest, feeling his pressure rising, and his oxygen threatening to cut off at any moment. As sweat poured down his forehead and neck, he didn't remember ever being this unsteady.

"Sir, are you ready?"

"Uh . . . yes. Go ahead."

His hands shook uncontrollably. He put them both in his pockets as he again looked down at the pool of blood, then quickly glanced at only the one side of her face that was exposed to him. It was distorted, cracked and bloody. He could barely identify her. But he knew. He was grateful her eye was closed.

After clearing his throat and blowing his nose, he found his voice. "This is Britt McKenzie, twenty-seven-years old. She . . . uh . . . resides. . . did reside upstairs in this condominium owned by Meg Carson. He pointed to the building next to the body.

The officer then handed him a document and pen. "Could you please sign this as the person who identified the body, and we will need the other information filled out later at the precinct."

After standing there for what seemed like hours but was only a few seconds, he finished filling out his name, address, and occupation, which was barely legible. That's when he stepped back and took one last look down at the sheet. For the first time, he noticed Britt's bright red heels she had worn just the other day at his home. Her toes at the opening tip of the shoes were pointing upward. One shoe had fallen off and was lying next to her foot.

Sadly, the sheet was not long enough to cover them. He turned to go back to his car.

Walking in the middle of the street, *he knew he would never lose that vision of his friend.* His heart skipped a few beats as he looked up to see Detectives Mason and Hall approaching him from the corner. He worked hard in that moment to contain not only his grief, but his anger.

"Our condolences to you and your family and friends." Detective Hall touched his arm lightly.

Detective Mason shook his head in agreement while writing something on a small pad of paper.

"Why didn't you tell me over the phone who I was coming to see lying on the ground in a pool of blood?"

His voice cracked. He pronounced every word with gritted teeth, then stared at Detective Mason, who had just lifted his head.

Detective Hall spoke up. "We had another emergency call on top of Britt McKenzie's death. An officer yelled to me the urgency, and I had to pick it up. We had planned to be back here in time to catch you before giving the identification. I apologize, Michael."

Detective Mason spoke up, "We are sorry your friend became a victim. We will investigate until we know exactly what happened here."

"Victim? You're labeling this a homicide? What about a suicide?"

Detective Mason put his large hand on Michael's shoulder. "We're not sure yet. As you know, gathering all the evidence takes time when there is no suspect on the scene. In this case, we need witnesses. To wait and see if it is not a homicide is not how we work. We want to be sure we know exactly how and why this happened."

"Time is important also," Detective Hall continued. "We would appreciate it if you and Mrs. Carson could come to the precinct tonight to answer questions. You both knew the deceased. Eight-thirty?"

"Sure." Michael turned and walked toward his car. He couldn't wait to get out of there. He hurried back up the street, trying to remember the last time he had cried. He held it back until he reached his vehicle. Believing this was a suicide, never had he imagined that Britt was that unstable. He regretted he couldn't have saved her.

When he reached his car, he blotted his eyes with a tissue from his glove compartment. He then picked up the phone to call Meg. *He dreaded giving her the bad news.*

CHAPTER EIGHT

Philadelphia, PA

At Charlie and Laney's condo, about forty minutes after their friends had arrived, Meg's phone buzzed. She excused herself from the table and walked over to view the other high-rise buildings through their floor-to-ceiling windows. "Hi Michael. What's going on?"

In seconds, she was sobbing and holding her head. Charlie ran over and took the phone from her. Their dog laid next to her feet.

"Hi, Uncle Mike. What's happening?" As he listened, he looked over at both mother and daughter consoling one another.

"I'm afraid Britt is dead."

Charlie couldn't respond at first. Then asked, "How?"

"She either jumped from Meg's front terrace down the three stories or it could be a homicide. The detectives are not yet sure." He breathed deeply, then continued. "An older woman across the street from Meg's condo called the police. From her terrace she noticed a woman lying in a pool of blood on the pavement and she was not moving. The police took down her information when they arrived on the scene. Meg's condominium is now off-limits until they give the all-clear. In fact, the whole street is blocked off with police everywhere."

"Poor Britt. Are you there now?"

"Yes." Michael's voice broke again. He cleared his throat. "Can you keep Meg at your place for a while? In fact, let her know she will have to stay over there at least for one night. Tell her we have to be at the precinct tonight at eight-thirty p.m. The detectives want to question us."

"No problem."

"I'm leaving here now and will be there shortly."

"Okay, Uncle Mike. See you soon."

Michael was so heartbroken he couldn't save his friend he got into his car and took off to a local pub in the city. He ordered a double Scotch on the rocks to relax him. The bar was filling up, but he didn't care. His mind was on his son and Britt. Before leaving about an hour later, he did get a little something to eat so he wouldn't appear inebriated when he met up with the detectives later. When he reached the car, his phone lit up again. This time it was Detective Mason.

"I'm afraid we have more news. Our police officers are presently looking for Ben. Any information about his whereabouts you can provide will help my officers find him. We need to question Ben as soon as possible. We will let you know when we have him here."

Michael could barely reply in a normal voice. "Is he charged with something?"

"We are not sure yet. We'll talk when you get here later. In the meantime, if you know where he is or he contacts you, please call us."

"I will." He ended the call, realizing he wasn't about to pull more information from the detective. He hit Charlie's number.

"Hi again, Uncle Mike."

"Can you put Meg on the phone?" Michael could feel his blood pressure rising. He now had a headache he had gotten rid of earlier.

"Sure." Charlie handed the phone to Meg. "It's Uncle Mike."

She walked toward the windows again for privacy. "Hi Michael."

"I'm sorry about Britt. But I have to ask if you noticed anything out of the ordinary today before or when you left your condo to drive to Charlie and Laney's?" *He took a deep breath and held it, hoping she wouldn't say what he was thinking.* While waiting, he lit a cigarette from the glove compartment.

"I apologize for not mentioning this sooner, but it left my mind until Detective Hall called here a little while ago. She asked if I saw anyone on my street who looked suspicious today or came to my condo. I was so upset after hearing about Britt's . . . you know, I didn't want to lie so I told her Ben was on the street. I was driving away from my condo and he and someone else at the wheel had parked right next to my car stopped in the line of traffic. I peered into Ben's face, but I don't think he recognized me. He looked away quickly and headed up the street."

"Which way? Did he walk toward your condo or in the other direction?" There was silence for what seemed like forever. Then she spoke in a weak voice, almost crying. "Towards my condo. I couldn't see past the cars behind me so I can't say where he went at that point. Why are you asking?"

Covering his eyes with his hand, Michael asked, "Has he ever been to your place before, Meg?"

"Not that I'm aware. I can't be sure. I'm not always there, you know?"

"Detective Mason has his men looking for my son. I will have to find him before the police. I need to know why they want him. They expect us at the precinct at eight-thirty tonight for questioning. Can I pick you up at eight?"

"I'll be ready. I'm sure Ben wouldn't be involved in something like this."

"Stay calm and tell them the truth when we are questioned, Meg. See you soon." He had to lean out of his car and vomit into the gutter. The cigarette had been no help at all.

With his head pumping and his eyes burning, he ended the call and pressed Jessica's number.

"Have you seen Ben at all this week?"

"No. I told you that the last time we talked. Did you find him?"

"Don't worry, I will. Until then, if he comes home you must call me right away, Jessica. Do you understand?"

"Can you elaborate?" *At this point, he wanted to scream at her, but controlled himself.*

"Keep him there and call me without him knowing it. Will you do that?"

"Why? You are scaring me."

Michael's other line lit up. "I can't talk now. For our son's sake, please do as I ask." He switched to the other line.

"Detective Hall here. I am sorry to do this to you, but we are on our way to an emergency right now. It has nothing to do with Ben. Can we meet with the two of you tomorrow about noon, instead of tonight?"

"We'll see you then." Michael heaved a sigh of relief. *This would give him more time to search for his son.*

CHAPTER NINE

Bucks County, PA

The next morning, Michael awoke early with his son on his mind. He felt helpless that he couldn't find him. Now he would be brought in by the police.

Nicky came out of the bathroom. "Babe, you look terrible."

"Thanks. I needed that," he groused.

"Did you get any sleep? I heard you get up a few times during the night."

"Got a lot on my mind."

"I wish I could help in some way."

"Now that you mention it, I could use a back rub before I leave. Has Michaela left for school?"

"It's Saturday. She's out shopping with her friends. She is now fourteen, you know. Let's go. I will be happy to give you a work-over."

"That sounds a bit scary." He grabbed her and carried her up the stairs to the master bedroom. Then they ended up in the shower.

An hour later, after having breakfast together at home, his phone lit up. "Hey Nick."

"Sorry I didn't get right back to you. What's going on?"

"I'm afraid I have bad news. Britt is dead."

"What?"

"The detectives are not sure if she jumped from her deck or if it's a homicide. I hate to cut you off right now, but I was just about to leave for a funeral service. I'm already late, so can I give you the details later?"

"Sure. We are home from Paris so why don't you come by the house? It will be good to see you. Then you can fill us all in later."

"Great. I'll see you then."

"Whenever you arrive is fine. I'll let the ladies know."

"Thanks."

Shortly after, he and Nicky left the house for work. "I have a long day, so don't expect me for dinner. After the funeral service this morning, I must pick up Meg and get to the precinct. I'm glad they didn't make us come in last night, but I do know they are looking for Ben right now."

Nicky walked with him toward his car. "Do you have any ideas where he could be?"

"Not one. Jessica gave our maintenance workers some names and addresses to check out, but nothing yet. I have no idea what kind of evidence the detectives have on Ben." He gave her a kiss and got into the driver's seat of his car. "Get to work woman," he taunted. *He was proud of his partner, who was a Science and Biology Professor at Cobert University nearby. On Saturdays, she often held a class for students who needed extra help.*

He pulled out of their driveway after the love of his life and turned in the opposite direction on the road. With so much to worry about, he had driven about two miles from his home in Bucks County without noticing another car had been following him. The vehicle hit him in the rear fender. Glancing in his rearview mirror, he quickly pulled to the right—almost hitting a tree, when the black car sped up. This time, it slammed into his passenger side then tore off around him. Getting back on the road, Michael hit the gas, trying to catch up to the same car that had been tailing him for many months. But once again, the vehicle disappeared.

By the time he arrived at his funeral home in Philadelphia, his favorite person, his beautiful and bright daughter, Becky, greeted him. She was second in command in their business. She had been preparing for their morning service.

Michael put his things down on the desk and opened his arms. "Come here, my love." They hugged. "Are you sure you are still five feet, eight inches? You look about five-eleven now."

"Where have you been, Dad? I know you had the last two weeks off, but you're usually around here off and on. I missed you."

"I owe you an apology. You do a great job here. I'm grateful it allows me more time off. I missed you also and do have to talk to you about a few developments. How about dinner together tomorrow evening? You pick the

restaurant and make the reservations wherever you want to dine. I'm yours for the night."

"I accept." She gave him one of her dimpled smiles.

"Now, let's get this service moving. I have to leave here and find your brother."

"I haven't seen him either. Good luck."

When the service ended and everyone was gone, Michael checked with his workers to see if they had found information on Ben. To his disappointment, their response was negative.

"See you later, Becky. I love you," he yelled across the room to where she was cleaning up.

"I love you too, Dad. Catch you tomorrow night."

He took off to pick Meg up at Charlie and Laney's home. She came right down when he rang the doorbell.

He held the car door open for her and drove them to the Philadelphia Police Station.

"Tell me you found Ben."

"Afraid not. No one seems to have seen him."

"I can't believe Britt is gone. What a horrible thing to happen to such a wonderful young woman."

Michael didn't respond. He couldn't discuss it then. It was enough he had to talk to the detectives about her.

He pulled into the station lot, parked his car and held Meg's door open. Once inside, they only waited fifteen minutes for Detective Hall to greet them at the front desk. They were taken to a well-lit, small room with a table and some chairs.

Detective Mason stood when they entered the room. He shook Michael's hand. "We appreciate you coming in today."

As usual, Detective Hall placed the recorder in the center of the table between them. "We would like to interview you one at a time. Do either of you have a problem with that?"

"No," they both replied.

Meg turned toward Michael. "I'll go first. Maybe Ben will come in before your turn."

He winked at her, then followed Detective Hall to the cafeteria below, where he was able to collect his thoughts while enjoying their hot coffee and pastries.

He worried the entire time he spent in the cafeteria that his son was in great danger and he imagined all kinds of scenarios. *Ben could be tied up with the wrong crowd and ticked someone off,* he decided. He was relieved to hear his name called as Meg returned to take his seat and enjoy the goodies.

"Try the pastries," he advised.

He and the detective returned to the room where Detective Mason waited.

"We won't keep you long. Have a seat. Can you tell us how you knew Britt McKenzie?"

He hesitated a moment to gather his thoughts. "The Campanella's introduced us during the holidays a few months ago. We were both at their house for various events."

"How well would you say you have gotten to know her?" Detective Mason studied his face.

"Not well until she shared with me a relationship problem she was having. I tried to help her. That was just a few days ago. She showed up at my home in Bucks County, unannounced."

"What kind of problem did she have . . . abuse?"

"Nothing like that. Britt had an affair with a married man for only a few months. She was in love with this guy, and he recently told her their affair was over. He swore he would never leave his wife for her.

She was devastated and came to my place for advice, and to cry on my shoulder."

"Did she tell you who this guy was or give any real information about him?"

"No. I have no idea who he could be."

Detective Mason squinted his eyes and tilted his head before asking Michael, "Why do you suppose Britt came to you? Was it because of her connection to your brother, Matthew when he was alive?"

"Her connection?" *Michael's thoughts quickly turned to the jail cell he had spent so much time in for his brother's crimes. But why would the detective go there? Does he know about their relationship, his and Matthew's, before his brother died?*

Still waiting for a response, Detective Hall intervened. "You know, you are related to the man who Britt McKenzie dated for five years prior to his death."

"Oh, I see. The month before she arrived at my home that day, I helped her move from the Campanella's house in Cape May to Meg's condominium in Philadelphia, top floor. Meg had been trying to rent it out. It was perfect for Britt since she had plans to attend college in that area in Philadelphia come September. Meg was thrilled to have her as a tenant."

Detective Mason jotted something on his tablet, then picked up the questioning. "Do you know why she was living at Dana and Nick's home before that?"

Now he was getting the detective's train-of-thought. "Britt had taken a part-time job in their art gallery helping Nick care for the shop . . . especially when he couldn't be there. They felt it would be good for her to live with them since she had no family. She would be close to their art gallery. As you now know, Dana was sure you had the wrong man in prison. She was grateful to Britt for going to the prison with her to prove that I was not guilty of the crimes with which I was charged. Britt McKenzie proved it to you." He stopped to take a sip of water.

"Like I told you before, the Campanella's went to Paris late January for two months or so. I talked to Nick before coming here and learned they have returned home to Cape May today."

"The Campanella's were close to Britt then. Do you think their friendship started when the three of them visited the prison to see you?" Detective Mason asked.

"I suppose they could have bonded after that." He glanced down at his watch.

Detective Hall cut in so she could question Michael, "How was Britt's and Nick's relationship? Were they close?"

"I suppose as close as Dana was with Britt. It was her desire to bring Britt to their home while she was working the gallery. Nick's a nice guy, so he went along with the idea."

"We have held you long enough, Michael." Detective Mason stood, pushed his chair back and pressed the recorder off.

Detective Hall stopped him at the door. "Did Nick Campanella stay in Paris with his wife for those entire two months?"

"You would have to ask him that question."

Michael turned and left with Meg. He dropped her off at Charlie and Laney's condo. "You have keys?"

"Yes, I'll be fine. Please be careful on the road. I know you are under a lot of stress. Call me if you hear from Ben, will you?"

"I promise." Michael walked her to the front door. His chest felt heavy. Before pulling away, he reminded himself to breathe deeply a few times. He closed his eyes and did the breathing before hitting the road to Cape May, New Jersey as planned. He had a lot to discuss with his sister and brother-in-law. He also wanted to hear about their trip to Paris, and maybe even hold his niece, Emily Rose, who he was told is now four months old. Dana mentioned that their baby is rolling all over the floor and giggling a lot. He couldn't wait to see her.

CHAPTER TEN

Cape May, NJ

Late afternoon, Michael arrived at his sister's Victorian home at the Jersey Shore. He loved it there and leaned against the car while facing the ocean. The view of the glistening waves calmed him. The weather was sunny and warm. It felt like he was on vacation whenever he visited this family who has become so dear to him. He wondered if he would ever have this kind of peace in his life.

"Come on up," Nick yelled from the top of the many stairs leading up to their veranda. Once at the top, he hugged his brother-in-law. "I'm looking forward to this visit." Michael followed him into the house.

Dana, Louisa, Kate and Austin were all in the den. He gave everyone a hug. "Where's little Emily Rose?"

Dana made a sad face. "Sorry you missed her. She has been cranky since we left Paris. We think it's due to the flight home and her schedule being thrown off.

Our little darling is now taking a much-needed nap. I'm sure she'll be awake before you are leaving."

"Good. I'm happy to see all of you."

"Kate and Austin stopped by since we hadn't seen them either in two months."

"Then none of us have gotten together since the weddings," Michael guessed. "Kate, you and Laney were the most beautiful brides. It was clever of you to have everything in this house with the cold January weather at that time. Whose idea was that?"

"Charlie came up with that plan because both Laney and I wanted a quiet, small wedding in Cape May. This house has so many rooms and floors, that turning the art studio into the reception area, along with the view of the ocean across the road turned out to be a great idea."

"I agree. Congratulations again. I haven't had the time to stop by and see my nephew and his lovely wife, but I hope to before they have the baby."

Dana was all smiles. "We can't wait to be grandparents. I just hope that our new grandson is healthy when he arrives." All agreed.

Louisa looked over at her son. "So how are you holding up with all that is happening, Michael? We feel terrible about Britt's death. Do the detectives have a suspect?"

"Prepare yourself for my response to that question. Meg tells me that Ben was in Britt's apartment that day."

The shock on their faces caused his headache to return. "To my knowledge, the detectives do not have a suspect yet. If only I could get to my son and hear his side of the story. He's been missing for over two weeks now."

Louisa got up and walked around the table to hug him. "I'm sorry, Son. I wish we could help. I will be saying lots of prayers."

"Thanks, Mom. I appreciate it."

The others gave their best wishes that Ben had nothing to do with the murder of Britt McKenzie.

Nick put his hand on Michael's shoulder, "I'm sure he had a good reason for being at her apartment. He probably doesn't even know that she has died."

He felt comfortable telling them about his son's situation. After all, they are his family now.

"How are things going at the Bed and Breakfast?" Michael asked.

Austin responded, "I took a week's vacation to do more work on the place."

Nick got into the conversation. "I can't imagine that beautiful building needing any kind of work this soon."

"It's little things that bug my dear wife. Rather than hear about them daily, I will get the job done." They all laughed.

Nick added, "That's what I always say, Austin. 'Yes, Honey.' It keeps a smile on her lovely face and only takes a few hours from my life." He chuckled and Dana hugged him to her.

Michael had a grin on his face. "Smart husband. I'll have to remember that one. Not to change the subject, but I did want to mention Britt's funeral service. When her body is released, I would like to have the service at my funeral home . . . if that's okay with the two of you. I know you both did so much for Britt."

"Sure, Michael. We will pay for it," Dana offered.

"That's not necessary. Britt once shared with me that her wishes were to be cremated when her time came. I can take care of that after her service." *Then he alone would bury her urn of ashes next to Matthew's grave.*

Dana touched his arm. "Let us know the date and time when you will have the service. I'll get in touch with everyone."

"Thanks. I have one more thing to share. Then I want to hear about Paris and how your portrait turned out." He coughed a few times and sipped his drink before continuing. "I asked Jessica for a divorce." Silence filled the room. The faces of his family revealed their surprise with raised eyebrows, open mouths, huge pupils. *He knew he had a lot of explaining ahead.*

Nick shook his head. "I'm sorry to hear that, Michael. I never realized your marriage was in trouble."

"Without boring you all with what prompted this, I will say it's time I moved on from the charade of our marriage we kept for our children's sake. It did nothing for Ben. In fact, I will take the blame for his actions these days. I hadn't realized until now that both my children probably figured out a long time ago that Jessica and I were not together. We just lived in the same house and pretended we were happy when necessary."

"This is so sad." His mom had tears in her eyes.

"There is more that you might not understand, but I have to get it out because I want my 'other family' to be a part of yours eventually."

Nick's eyebrows raised. "Your other family?" All eyes on Michael, he felt the atmosphere change in the room as their postures tensed up.

"The lifestyle with Jessica changed decades ago. At that time, I was out at a party and met a woman by the name of Nicky Collins. She had promised the hostess she would be there, but she had never had alcohol before. By the time I had arrived at the party, she was sitting in a corner looking lost. I made conversation and could tell right away that she had a little too much to drink. Long story short, I drove her home. A few months later, I ran into her again. Nothing had changed between me and Jessica in fourteen years. So, I asked Nicky out on a date, then another, and we eventually moved in together. That's when I purchased our home in Bucks County, Pennsylvania."

No one spoke, so he continued. "A few years later, our daughter, Michaela came along. Since that time, I have been living two lives for the kids, I'm sorry to admit. But I didn't want my children to suffer. Now I realize they did because I was at one place or the other. Ben and Becky knew something was up."

"Excuse me," Louisa left the room and Kate followed her to the kitchen.

Dana looked back at Michael, "Of course this is a shock to us."

The silence after that lasted until Louisa and Kate returned from the kitchen with hot coffee and danish. Nick had left for the bathroom.

"I would hope we can all embrace your new family and be happy to get to know them," Louisa poured the coffee into the cups.

"How old is Michaela?" Kate asked while placing the dishes on the table.

"She just turned fourteen. She is excited that I am home now and sleeping in the same house. She had been told all these years that I worked outside of the state during the week and could only be home on weekends."

"That must have been rough on everyone. I know *I* couldn't handle two separate families," Nick admitted.

"You better never try, Buddy!" Dana pulled his ear.

Austin cleared his throat, "I have to ask you how Jessica responded to all this."

"She's fine with it, as she should be, and that's all I'll say."

"When can we meet Nicky and Michaela?" Louisa asked.

"Maybe I could bring them to Jake's surprise party you are planning. Of course, I'd bring Becky also."

Dana's face lit up. "That's a great idea. You can leave the address so I will know where to send the invitations to you all. I can't wait to meet them."

"When are you planning to tell Ben?" Louisa asked.

"I won't tell him right away when I find him. Becky and I have a dinner date tonight, which is when I will break the news to her. My guess is that she won't be shocked at all. As you know, my daughter with Jessica is twenty-eight now and has lived with us all these years at our funeral home apartment."

"She runs your business well," Dana noted.

"Becky deserves the business when I retire one day. I am glad Jessica agreed. Enough about me. Can I look in on Emily Rose now, Dana? I promise not to wake her. Then you can fill me in on your experiences in Paris before I have to dash out of here."

"Sure, let's go upstairs." She took the lead.

CHAPTER ELEVEN

Philadelphia, PA

Two weeks after Britt's death, the Philadelphia Detectives on the case had just finished dinner in the cafeteria at the precinct when they received a call. A gentleman reported that he had just returned from a week's vacation when a neighbor told him about the murder on his street.

Jim Cash stated that he had left that same night for his trip after picking up a suit at the cleaners on their corner. On his way back to his condominium, he had witnessed a young man outside the building where now he is told a murder took place. Before he had left for vacation, he had passed by their building and noted that a young woman had opened the door slightly. He stopped to say hello to them. The young man turned and looked right at him, so he knew he could identify him. The detectives asked him if he could come into the precinct right away so they could record his report.

When Jim Cash arrived at the station, he gave his identification to the desk officer. Detective Mason came right over and shook his hand.

"Good to meet you, Mr. Cash."

"Same here." He was led to a room where they question eyewitnesses.

"Take a seat." The detective placed a recorder in the center of the table.

"We have to record this."

"That's fine with me."

Detective Hall came through the door. "How's retirement treating you?" She shook hands with Mr. Cash.

"Great. I've been traveling. But I am glad to be home to help out with this case."

Detective Mason asked, "How do you two know one another?"

"Jim is a retired police officer. He worked in our precinct for years. You didn't arrive, Brock, until a year or so after Jim retired."

"Good to know." He pressed the button on the recorder. "Okay, let's have it, Mr. Cash. What did you witness the day of Britt McKenzie's death?"

"Call me Jim. Like I mentioned over the phone, I walked past the condominium across from mine. I noticed a man and a woman at that condo doorway where the crime took place later. The young man was standing on the pavement facing the front door that was partially open. I stopped to say hello and he turned and looked right at me." He took a swig of water, then continued. "'Can I help you?' the young man asked."

"I replied, 'I thought you might be new to the neighborhood and wanted to welcome you.'"

"'I'm visiting if that's okay with you.'" He sounded irritated.

"No problem," I told him and turned away to cross the street. By the time I walked up three floors to my apartment and hung up my suit, I heard a woman screaming. I went out to my terrace and looked over to where the same couple was on their terrace fighting. The young man I had given a hello to on the street minutes earlier was pulling the young woman's arms and yelling back at her."

"As a retired police officer, why didn't you call it in?" Detective Mason asked.

"They didn't stay out there long enough for me to run down or call the police. They lowered their voices and within minutes went back inside. I figured it was a lover's quarrel and they were making up. After, I left for my short vacation. When I went out to the car, I didn't hear a sound coming from their condo, so I pulled away from the curb. There was nothing outside of their apartment—especially not a body. But when I returned home, my neighbor, an older woman who I believe contacted your precinct when she witnessed a body on the pavement, told me about the crime. I thought my information might be of some help."

Detective Hall asked, "Did you see anyone else who might have looked suspicious go into their condominium at that time?"

"No one . . . not while I was still around. Like I told you, I left almost right away after things calmed down."

"Do you think you could pick this guy you saw at the condominium out of our database?"

"I'm willing to try."

Detective Hall stood. "Let's go. I'll take you downstairs."

Jim Cash followed her to a large room with a lot of activity, and people working with technology. She introduced him to the gentleman in charge there who gave Mr. Cash a seat and got him started. She watched as he studied the slides that were alphabetized. When he was in the P's, he pointed at Ben Pearson's mugshot. "He's your guy."

The detective asked again, "Are you sure?"

"One hundred percent. This guy not only showed me his face, but he spoke and in an angry tone I might add, which I could probably identify if I needed to in the future."

"Okay. Let's get back upstairs to finish up with you signing an affidavit, and other information we may need from you, Jim."

After Mr. Cash left the building, Detective Mason turned to his partner.

"Besides Jim Cash, don't forget Meg Carson witnessed Ben going toward her condo during the day of Britt's death."

Carla shook her head. "Since forensics already had Ben's DNA from the robbery a few months ago when they booked him for his first crime, I'm sure they can connect him to the evidence. For instance, with his shoe prints; fingerprints; hair from a struggle, etc. We need it right away though."

"I'll call over to my brother and have him put a rush on it."

"Good thinking, Brock. He *is* at the top and should have enough pull. Have you ever asked him to do this before?"

"Never. I'm sure he'll realize how important timing is right now." He picked up the business phone.

She walked out of the room to grab their mail down the hallway. She was waiting for something important. When she returned, her partner was placing the receiver back on the business phone.

"What did he say?"

"He put three people on it. We should have it by tomorrow morning, or at least by noon."

******

Oblivious to all that was happening at the Philadelphia Police Department, Michael was having dinner with his daughter, Becky. After they finished their meal, they ordered cocktails. He reached across the table to touch his daughter's hand. "I have made some changes I need to discuss with you."

"To the funeral home?"

"Not exactly. The other day, I asked your mother for a divorce."

He gave her time to process his words, but she didn't seem surprised.

Putting her drink down, she studied his face. "Dad, this has been a long time coming. You don't really think it shocks me, do you?"

"I'm sorry, Honey. I didn't realize how much you suffered since you are the oldest, and that you might have caught on to our pretense of having a happy marriage. Then there's Ben who has been acting out, losing school, doing drugs, and all kinds of things. I believe he would never have done all this if he didn't recently see through the secrets."

"Mom's affair has been going on for a long, long time, as I am sure you know, Dad. She confided in me years ago about Roger. I wasn't happy with it, but I never wanted you to know because I thought it would hurt you."

"It did for many years, but I didn't want to break up the family while you and Ben were still young."

"I remember praying that you knew and just didn't share it, so you would feel free to have someone to love besides me and Ben."

"You are so caring and sweet, Becky. You and your brother kept my spirits up. After I learned fourteen years or so ago about your mom's affair, I ran into a wonderful woman at a party who needed help getting home. Her name is Nicky Collins. I think you will grow to love her too. Now, here's the big one, we have been together for over fourteen years."

"I am shocked as to how you pulled that off, Dad. I am very happy that you found love. Where have you been hiding her?"

"Once we decided we wanted to be together, I purchased a home in Bucks County. Nicky moved in there and I moved in some of my things periodically. Then a year later, we had Michaela, our daughter. You have a half-sister, Becky."

"A sister? Wow, that's such exciting news! She jumped up to hug her dad, spilling her drink on the floor. She took her seat again. "I have to be honest with you. I am glad this happened for you and mom. I have been so anxious at times, worrying about you both. When can I meet Nicky and Michaela?"

"I'll set it up. Our home will always be yours as well. They are hoping

to meet you too. I have always talked about how wonderful you are as a daughter, and as a business partner in the funeral home. Thanks for understanding. I love you."

"I love you more, Dad. I do have to ask though. How did you manage two homes and two families?

"Yeh, that was rough at times, but that's where I was on weekends and you and Ben were supposed to think I was working somewhere else. Michaela only got to see me then, so she was told by Nicky that my job took me far away during the week. I could only get home on weekends. We detested the lying, but I had no other solution at the time. Now we are all together, and I want you and your brother to be a big part of Michaela's life too."

"You've got my vote."

"Thanks, Honey. It's getting late." He motioned the waiter over to the table to take his credit card.

"I better get you home. I believe we have a busy day tomorrow. It's wonderful spending time with you, Becky. We should do this more often."

"I agree," she gave her dad a thumbs up.

They drove the short distance to the funeral home where he dropped his daughter off. He got out and held her to him. "Thank you, Becky, for accepting all of this news so graciously. I am blessed to have you as a daughter. I was so worried as to how this would affect you, Honey."

"Dad, you know how much I love you. Why would I not be accepting of having a real sister in my life? This is amazing. Of course, I am happy for you. Watching you all those years trying to be a good husband, not knowing your

wife was cheating on you was not your fault. You deserve more than that. I am happy you have found love." She hugged him as tight as she could.

"Thank you, Sweetheart. You warm my heart. Now get some sleep." They hugged once again, then he watched his daughter go into the funeral home apartment before driving away.

CHAPTER TWELVE

Philadelphia, PA

Brock walked over to the board in their office at the precinct. "Let's go over this evidence we now have on Ben Pearson from the crime lab technician's findings, Carla." She joined him at the board. "Let's face it . . . the kid had a motive. He believed his dad was having an affair with Britt McKenzie, was angry about it, and he confronted her to save his family."

"Could be considered a 'Crime of Passion'."

"Brock, we know he is incorrigible; disappears from home for weeks at a time, dropped out of school, and still ingests drugs. Most mentionable is that he probably shared the Methamphetamine with the deceased."

"We have quite a bit of evidence against Ben," Brock stated. "Then there's the eyewitness testimony from the neighbor across the street, Jim Cash. He picked him out of the database and had been face-to-face with Pearson outside Meg's condominium. With what forensics gathered at the crime scene, we have more than probable cause to pick him up and interrogate him."

"Agreed. We also have his fingerprints on the bottle of whisky and on doorknobs and other areas in her apartment. But let's not forget what your brother sent over to us, which includes other sets of prints besides Ben's from Britt's apartment in the condominium."

"True," Brock acknowledged. "We have a lot of work to do." He then pointed out, "Britt had a small amount of the Methamphetamine in her system when examined, but there was none in the apart-ment. We know that Ben was brought in here before with it in his pocket."

"Do you want more coffee?" Carla offered.

"You could make a fresh pot if you wish. I'll have some when I get back from picking up the warrant."

Before leaving their office, he pushed a button on the business phone. "Jonas put out an APB on Ben Pearson. I want him in this office for interrogation. He is probably somewhere in Philadelphia. He's Cau-casian, five-foot-five, blonde unruly hair, and most likely a bit drugged up. He might be hanging out with one of the gangs. He can be difficult but don't hurt him. Read him his rights and get him in here."

Next, he called Michael. "I have some news. We haven't found your son, but he is now our number one suspect in Britt McKenzie's case. My officers are looking for him for interrogation. Prepare your lawyer. I'm giving you a heads-up. I'll let you know as soon as we find him."

"I don't understand. How is he your main suspect?"

"We'll explain all that when we get him in here. I will call you at that time."

"Okay, thanks." Michael jumped into his car and began searching again for his son. He checked as many hangouts as he could find. He did not find Ben. He had spent hours checking out all the shelters in the Philadelphia area—still nothing. Tired, he finally hit the last shelter where he was told his son had been. The guy who runs the shelter told Michael, "He spent two nights here, and then a gang came along and dragged him into a car."

"What's the name of the gang?"

The guy who ran the shelter did not offer much information. His response to Michael was, "I don't know. If I did, I wouldn't say. It's a good way to get killed." He shut the door in his face. Michael got into his car and called the precinct right away. "I need to speak with one of your detectives." He could barely keep his dreaded thoughts inside his head while he waited. His heart was pumping harder than usual.

"Detective Hall."

"Michael Pearson. I found out Ben was staying in a shelter and just recently a gang came and dragged him into their car. The guy at the shelter was scared to give me the name of the gang. I'm terrified for my son's life right now."

"Okay, calm down. We will find him and call you right away," she assured him. Michael ended the call and could feel his muscles tightening like a noose.

CHAPTER THIRTEEN

Philadelphia, PA

T

he medical examiner released Britt McKenzie's body to Michael Pearson's funeral home a week later. The next day friends arrived to pay their respects, including Charlie and Laney, and Nick's brother Tony and his wife, Paula. Jake and his family came down from the Pocono Mountains to attend the service. Dana and her family were there also, along with Kate and Austin.

It was a very cold day, filled with rain and angry clouds. *Dana thought back to the day they had all tossed her dad's ashes over the waves of the ocean at the Jersey shore. It had been his final request. The weather had been cold with clear skies and snowflakes dropping to the ground.*

She was brought back to reality by the prayer for Britt's spirit. She looked around the room at the beautiful flowers from friends who could not make the service. She had introduced herself to the few friends Britt had that no one there really knew. They were sweet, and she could tell they loved Britt in their own way, even though they didn't see her often.

Once the priest finished talking, music filled the room and their daughter, Emily Rose began to hum. She loved music, and at five-months-old, she tried to make the sounds she heard while sitting on her daddy's lap. Although their baby wasn't a wild child, she did have moments of joyful outbursts. Dana was grateful their little one had been quiet up to that point.

After the service, Michael spoke at the podium, "I want to thank you all for coming today. I know Ms. McKenzie would have been shocked at the number of people here who really cared about her. She lived a short, challenging life, but we can take solace in the fact that she is now at peace." He took a moment to look out at the number of people there for Britt.

"In a conversation about death, when someone close to both of us had died, I remember Britt stating to me her wishes for cremation only. She wanted it to be private. I would ask each of you to walk around the casket now if you wish to say your goodbyes. Then you may leave by the parking lot exit. Thank you for coming."

Dana was relieved that they didn't have to witness the cremation. She had to do that once years ago for someone close to her and it tore her apart.

"I'll carry Emily Rose while you pull the car up, Nick." She took their daughter from her husband's lap and left the church.

After all the goodbyes, they reached the sidewalk just as their car arrived. A little boy stood nearby with his family. To Dana's amazement, their daughter could not resist a giggle and flashed her eyelashes toward him.

As Dana got into the passenger side of the car after Emily Rose was strapped in her seat in the back, she laughed again. "Our daughter is already

boy crazy, Honey." It lightened up a very solemn morning. Nick winked at his little daughter.

Before they pulled out, Michael stopped at the Campanella's car window. "I thought I'd mention I got a call from the detectives that they are looking for Ben and will be bringing him in for interrogation. I'll be in touch and let you know what happens. I hope they don't believe Ben is Britt's murderer."

Dana reached for Michael's hand. "Stay strong. There's a good possibility that Ben was not at the condominium when Britt made a choice to jump to her death. Please, hold on to that thought. It's a terrible one, but it would prove his innocence."

"Thanks, Sis. You always seem to put things in perspective . . . even the worst scenarios. Drive carefully."

After everyone left, Michael talked with his grave diggers and gave them a date when they would go to his home grounds in Bucks County where they buried his brother and dig a grave next to it for Britt McKenzie's urn. He then took off to try and find his son before the police. But when his phone lit up and he saw the name, he knew he was too late.

"Detective?"

"My men found your son in a shelter in Philadelphia. They are bringing him in now. We will hold the interrogation at three p.m. Did you notify your lawyer?"

"Yes. He'll be with us. Is Ben okay?"

"Let's wait to talk when you come in later. I'm told he is calm and didn't give the officers any problem. They read him his Miranda rights, but we will

do that again here since he is a minor. I want him to understand the implications involved if he chooses to talk. See you then."

"Thanks. We'll see you at three." He steeled himself and called Jessica to prepare her.

CHAPTER FOURTEEN

Philadelphia, PA

Michael picked Jessica up and drove to the Philadelphia Police Department for their son's interrogation for the murder of Britt McKenzie. They had little to say to one another on the drive there, each with their own thoughts.

When they arrived, he parked and held the passenger side door open for Jessica. They entered the building, both in a bundle of nerves. His almost ex-wife pushed her hair back first, then twisted her hands together. He could feel his heart thumping extra hard in anticipation of what this process would reveal.

They both sat in the chairs behind the front desk after signing in with the officer on duty. He assured them one of the detectives would be along.

"Mr. and Mrs. Pearson follow me please," Detective Hall directed after she shook their hands. "I know this is tough on both of you as parents, but we work very hard to get the truth out of juveniles. You will have time with him after. Do you have any questions?"

"Does he know we are here?" Jessica asked.

"No. If he asks that question, we will tell him you are here. Otherwise, we do not offer that information. You will both be behind the one-way glass, and your lawyer is here now and will be in the room with your son. He spoke with Ben earlier."

"Thank you, detective."

"Okay. Let's get you both in place before we begin."

Detective Hall took them to the room where they could watch and hear all that transpired during their son's interrogation. They were given bottles of water, and if needed they could leave that room at any time. Detective Hall returned to the interrogation room where Detective Mason, Ben Pearson, and Michael's lawyer, Jack Barr had just entered.

Detective Mason took the lead when he pushed the button on the recorder in the center of the table. The detectives were sitting across from Ben and his lawyer.

"Mr. Pearson, we would like you to state your name, age, birthdate, and the address of where you live. It is now three p.m. on April 21, 2012."

The suspect tossed his head some and wiggled a bit in his chair before responding. "Ben Pearson. I'm sixteen-years-old. I live in Philadelphia, Pennsylvania where I was born."

Detective Hall took over. The detectives had agreed she might have more luck with him responding. They based that thinking on their visit to his home the day they had arrested his dad last year.

"Thank you." She kept a pleasant tone. "You were read your Miranda Rights when you were picked up by our police officers earlier today. Do you remember that Mr. Pearson?"

"Yes. Call me Ben."

"We would like to go over them one more time to be sure you fully understand your rights in a court of law, Ben."

"Okay."

"We will be asking you questions but you do have the right to remain silent. Do you understand that?"

"Yeh."

"If you choose to speak, you must realize that anything you say to us in this room today can be used against you."

"I get it." Ben shook one of his legs constantly.

"Your counsel, Mr. Barr, is here for you." The detective pointed to the lawyer. Ben shook his head in response.

"If you do speak to us, you can stop talking at any time. Do you fully understand all of your rights now?"

"Yes." He guzzled water from the bottle in front of him.

"Ben Pearson, you are being interrogated as a possible suspect for the murder of Britt McKenzie on March 12, 2012 at her apartment in Philadelphia, Pennsylvania."

"I did not kill Britt McKenzie! With his hands on the table, palms up, he tightened his fists. His lips were clamped down in anger as he stared at the detectives. "I didn't even know she was dead until your officers picked me up today."

This was the Ben Pearson they knew in the past who couldn't control his emotions when his dad had been arrested last year.

"Are you denying you were in Britt McKenzie's apartment on the day of the crime?"

"I was there. But I did not kill her!" He slammed his bare hand on the table, quickly pulling it back to his chest.

"Why were you at Britt McKenzie's apartment?" Detective Mason asked Ben.

He hesitated for a moment, but in a clear voice he did respond. "I was there because I thought she was having an affair with my dad. It upset me that he would do that to my mom. I wanted to let Britt know that I knew about their affair, and it had to be over. She had to agree to stop it before I left her place."

"Or else? Did you give her an ultimatum—a threat of what you would do to her?"

"Of course not. She wasn't going to let me in her apartment, so I may have pushed my way up the stairs. I told her I would let my mother know about the affair she was having with my dad even if it hurt her. I figured Britt wouldn't want that to happen."

"So, you went there to keep her away from your dad, and it didn't work out how you thought it would. You fought back-and-forth. I'm sure you didn't mean it, but your anger took over and you pushed Ms. McKenzie over the terrace to her death."

"That's not what happened!" Now his voice was rising.

"I hear you, Ben. These things happen in a moment of passion. You were worried so much about your mom and dad's situation that your anger got out-of-control," Detective Mason studied the boy's face and body language.

Ben's head dropped down. He shook it from side-to-side. There was no other movement or sound during those few seconds. His attorney leaned over and whispered something to him. Then Ben raised his head.

"There is no way I would ever kill anyone, even if I was angry. Britt was fine when I left her apartment. Once I realized that she was just friends with my dad, I even sat there longer while she went into the bathroom. Right before that, she had a bottle of whisky under her sofa where she had been sitting when things calmed down. She pulled it up and downed quite a bit of it before I grabbed the bottle from her hand. I stayed at her apartment until she came out of the bath, and I knew she was okay. Britt told me to get out. She was very much alive when I left her place."

"You had Methamphetamine on you when our officers picked you up today. Did you share that with Ms. McKenzie?"

Ben stated, "Yes, I did give her a small amount of meth, thinking it might calm her."

"Where did you go when you left the building?"

"Down the street to my friend's car. I got in and we took off for his house in northeast Philadelphia."

"Your friend's name?"

"Josh Janzy. He has nothing to do with this. I asked him for a ride up and back and he agreed. He stayed in the car the whole time as far as I know."

"Is there anything more you'd like to share with us, Ben?" Detective Mason asked.

His finger went up to his eye, he thought for a moment, then replied, "No, I told you all I know and it's the truth." Ben held his stare at the detective when he answered.

"Are you denying that you killed Britt McKenzie in a heat of passion?"

"I did not kill Britt McKenzie!" Ben loudly announced.

Detective Mason pushed a number on the business phone. Within seconds a woman in plain clothes appeared at the door. The detective turned the recorder off and handed it to her. She left right away.

Detective Hall looked over at Ben. "Your parents will be in shortly to spend time with you." The detective picked up the business phone. "Can you please bring Mr. and Mrs. Pearson into the interrogation room now?"

When the couple entered the room, they each hugged their son tightly and took a seat across from him at the table. There was an officer outside the door.

The detectives left with Ben's attorney. They went into another room nearby to look over the information Ben Pearson had given them while insisting he was not guilty of Britt McKenzie's death. It was now in print, word-for-word from the recorder that was used in the interrogation. Next, they would get Ben Pearson's signature on it.

Michael's lawyer had a different attitude about Ben's responses. "I think my client did well with the questioning."

Detective Mason did not agree. "I believe his anger issues and bully tactics haven't left him yet. He did better than we expected. However, we have to hold him until we hear from forensics and look into others who could tell us more about Ben, like his friend who drives him around. Young Mr. Pearson is a flight risk, a drug addict, and as you witnessed, he has some pent-up anger. As you know, this is not his first crime," Detective Mason stated.

"True. That does not mean he is a killer."

"We are investigating other suspects and questioning quite a few sources and witnesses in the case. Note that we will be on top of Ben's situation. None of us want to see him in a jail cell for long if he is innocent of this crime. Although almost all the evidence points to him being in Britt McKenzie's apartment that day." The detective got up from his chair. He and the lawyer shook hands. "I'll return in about ten minutes to bring you in on the signing of Ben's confession. Here's today's news if you haven't read it yet." The detective handed the newspaper to him and left the room.

Down the hall, Michael and Jessica were trying to assure their son that he won't be in jail for long.

"I'm not guilty of Britt's death, Dad."

"You have to be patient, Son."

"The reason I'm in this mess is because I was trying to save you from hurting mom." He stood with his arms flailing around as he spoke loudly. "You're the reason I'm in here!" Tears rolled down his cheeks. "I don't want you guys to get a divorce." He flung himself back down onto the bed.

"Who mentioned getting a divorce?" Jessica handed him a tissue.

"I thought dad was cheating on you. I went to his other house to spy on him. When I saw Britt there, and she kissed dad on the cheek, I thought they were having an affair."

"What other house?" Jessica asked, her eyes wide.

Michael glanced at her and shook his head no. "We'll discuss that later. Is that why you went to Britt's apartment, Ben?"

"Yes. At first, I accused her. Then we got into an argument and stuff, but eventually I believed she was just your friend and not a slut. I didn't kill her. You have to believe me," he yelled as he put his wet face in his hands.

Jessica rushed around the table and hugged her son. They sat quietly until he calmed down.

Michael spoke first, "Mr. Barr is working on getting you out of here. If you are telling the truth, and I believe you are, it will come out and the real killer will be caught. It might take a few days."

The door opened and the detectives came into the room with Mr. Barr behind them. Detective Hall placed a pen on the table in front of Ben with his confession printed out on a legal document.

"Please sign at the bottom of the page and fill out the rest of the information."

When the form was complete and checked over by his lawyer, Ben's parents hugged him before the police officer took him down the hall to their jail cell.

"Hang in there, Buddy. You'll be out soon," Michael hollered.

After saying goodbye to the Pearson's and Mr. Barr, Carla suggested she and Brock go to dinner before they question Ben's friend, Josh Janzy. She grabbed their coats. They left the precinct with hope they could clear Ben Pearson.

CHAPTER FIFTEEN

Philadelphia, PA

"I'm Detective Hall." She extended her hand to the woman inside the front door of their building.

"Janice Janzy." They shook hands. "This is my son, Josh."

"Hello. Thank you both for coming in to answer a few questions. Follow me to where we can talk privately."

They walked through a long hallway to a small room with a desk and four chairs. Detective Hall held the door open for them. "This is Mrs. Janzy and Josh Janzy."

Detective Mason," he shook their hands. "Have a seat. We won't keep you long." He then pointed to the recorder in the middle of the table. "We will have to record whatever you tell us here today."

"That's fine."

Detective Mason began. "Josh, we understand you and Ben Pearson are good friends. We have learned that you drove Ben to Britt McKenzie's condominium here in the city. Is that correct?"

"Yes Sir. He doesn't drive yet and told me he had to speak with a woman, so I offered to drive him there." His voice was a bit shaky. He looked over at his mother after he spoke. She smiled at him.

"When you arrived there, did you go into Ms. McKenzie's apartment with Ben, or did you stay in your vehicle?"

"I waited in the car for him, Sir. I had brought a book with me, which I always do. I get bored easily."

"You didn't leave your car the entire time Ben Pearson was inside Ms. McKenzie's apartment building?"

"No Sir. He asked me to wait in the car so I could drive him home."

"Were you parked right outside of the building Mr. Pearson entered?"

"No Sir. There were a lot of cars on the street. I found a spot about three buildings away."

"I see." The detective jotted down a few thoughts while Josh answered. He continued the questioning. "It sounds as if you and Ben drive around a lot together. Is that a fair assumption?"

"Not a lot. If he needs a ride and I'm available, I take him. We have been friends all through school."

Detective Hall interjected, "Josh, when Ben returned to your car from Meg's apartment, did you notice the time?"

His mother smiled at him again.

"I know I'm a nerd, but I am always aware of the time. It was exactly 4:03 p.m. when Ben returned and got into my car."

"Did he tell you anything that happened in Ms. Mckenzie's apartment or have anything else to say?"

"Only . . .'Get us out of here.'

"Did he seem anxious or angry?"

"Um . . . maybe anxious and annoyed."

"You told us you drive Ben around when he needs a ride. Maybe you could tell us why Ben asked you to take him to a home in Bucks County, Pennsylvania recently." Detective Mason did not take his eyes off Josh. He waited for the boy's response while he noted the need to look over at his mother once again. Then Josh dropped his head.

"Are you okay?" Detective Hall asked. "Take your time. You are in no trouble. We are trying to help your friend by understanding how he ended up at Britt McKenzie's home."

"I . . . uh, drove him up there to follow his dad and find out where he went every weekend."

"Why would he want to follow his dad? Was he worried about him?"

Detective Mason took over again. "It may help Ben's case if you continue to tell the truth, Josh."

"Okay. He thought his dad was cheating on his mom. He has been upset about that for some time. That morning, he asked me if I would pick him up early, so we could follow his dad."

"What happened when you arrived at Mr. Pearson's home in Bucks County? Did he know you were following him?"

"No. We hid in the bushes. There were so many trees, we figured there's no way he would know we were there."

"What was your plan once you were hidden?"

"Ben wanted to be sure his dad didn't have another woman. When we got there, he had the first shock—to learn his dad had another home."

"Then what happened?"

"When he discovered a woman was there talking to his dad, he went crazy."

"Did Ben know the woman?"

"Yes, but I don't think he knew her well. He told me later that he met her a few times at his aunt and uncle's house in Cape May, New Jersey."

"Were you able to hear their conversation?"

"No. They were in an enclosed patio. We could only see them, but they didn't see us. Then when the woman, who Ben called Britt, was ready to leave, they came out walking closer to where we were hiding. That's when we watched her kiss Ben's dad on his cheek. That put him into more of a rage. I tried to cover his mouth as I dragged him through the shrubbery."

"What happened next?"

"We ran through the trees and down the road to get into my car. We hopped in and I drove out of there as fast as I could. Ben told me later that the woman saw us. She was ready to turn out of the driveway to the road just as I sped past her. If my car had a faster start, she might not have seen him."

Detective Hall asked, "How was Ben on the way home . . . angry?"

"He was upset because what he suspected did happen."

"Did he then ask you to drive him to Britt McKenzie's the next day?"

"Yes."

"How was his mood when you got to Ms. McKenzie's place?"

"He seemed irritated that I leaned over and placed my hand on his shoulder to make him feel it would be okay. He pushed me away. He did say he wanted to make it clear to her that their affair had to stop, or he would tell his mother. I think he tried to act cool but ended up acting really anxious." He glanced at his mom.

"It's okay, Honey. You are doing right by your friend. I'm proud of you."

"Your mother is correct. We thank you for your honesty and for being concerned about your friend's welfare. I hope we didn't keep you too long." Detective Mason stood up and shook Josh's hand. "You have been a big help. Thank you both."

Detective Hall walked them to the front of the building and returned to their office where Brock filled two mugs with coffee. He handed one to his partner. "I'm about to believe you are right that it is possible Ben Pearson is innocent. I think it's time we talked to his parents about placing him in a locked down rehabilitation facility for juveniles with drug addictions and anger issues."

"I agree. That will help him more than sitting in a jail cell. I also think his friend, Josh, told us the truth today. His story was similar to Ben's, don't you think?"

"Yes. But we can't totally release him from this case and put him back on the street until we are one hundred percent sure he is innocent. I'd like to investigate further with the possibility that whomever Britt McKenzie was dating might have had enough of her and is the killer."

"After this coffee, I'm on my way home. I will contact the rehabilitation center tomorrow morning-- the one we discussed and feel it would be the best for

Ben. I already checked them out online. They have intake staff who will make the admissions process smooth and easy for the parents to understand. They have a team to help the family learn how their facility works. Once I explain Ben's situation, I will then contact Michael and Jessica and see if they agree with this facility for their son. We can set up the time since we will be using a few of our officers to escort Ben there."

"Good. Then we can get out of here and begin questioning the neighbors again to see if any of them noticed a male other than Ben, going or coming from Meg's condominium the day of McKenzie's death."

"Good idea, Carla. Did I tell you how well you handled Ben today? Your questioning was impressive also with some I hadn't thought to ask."

"As always Brock, let me say this, flattery will get you nothing." She laughed as she grabbed her briefcase and took off out of the room.

Detective Mason went over to their board on the wall which held all the photos they had so far. He drew a line from Britt McKenzie's face to Nick Campanella's and placed a question mark beside it.

CHAPTER SIXTEEN

Bucks County, PA & Philadelphia, PA

Michael Pearson hadn't slept well after witnessing the trouble Ben was having with the law. He knew his son had anger issues. The fact that he didn't have the time most days to interact with his son didn't help either. Yet, he did not believe Ben could push a woman over an outside terrace three stories down to her death. That was too much for his brain to compute. *Someone or something must be out there to prove his son's innocence. He would not stop searching until he found it.*

By the time he got out of bed, Nicky had already left for work. She was a thoughtful and caring person whose thinking was that it was better for him to get more sleep than be awakened for a kiss goodbye. He dragged himself into the shower, dressed, and ran downstairs. He grabbed the thermos of hot coffee she had left on the kitchen counter with a sweet note, and he headed for Philadelphia.

******

After the funeral service that morning, he received a call from Meg. She asked if he could stop by or meet her so she could get his opinion on a secret she had been keeping for a long time. He was eager to speak with his son again.

He knew Meg had been fretting over something big for a long time. So, he hurried over to her condominium first. But he was shocked to hear exactly how complicated a situation she had lived with all this time. He also wanted to check out the neighborhood to make sure the detectives hadn't missed anything that could clear Ben.

When he arrived at the police station, he parked his car and went in to ask for a visit with Ben. His son was not talking much and was still in pain from the beating he took. "How are you feeling physically?"

"I'm okay. I want to get out of here."

"Believe me, Son, I am working on it. I know you are innocent." He patted his head, held his tears for later, and gave Ben a big smile. I love you, Buddy. I would stay longer, but I want you to rest. You've been through a lot."

"Yeh." He put his head down on the pillow provided for him and faced the jail wall.

Michael left with the assurance to Ben he would be released soon.

Detective Mason stopped him as he left the building and was on the front steps. "Hello Michael. Detective Hall and I would like to place your son in a locked down rehabilitation facility. He would benefit much more from treatment than sitting in our jail cell. What do you think?"

"Wonderful. What brought this on?"

"Although we have evidence pointing to Ben as having been in Britt's condominium and sharing his drugs with her, we have learned from witnesses that your son left the building and the area before Britt's time-of-death."

"Thank God!"

"He is not home free yet, but we are working on it and still questioning neighbors and shops in the area."

"It's progress. I am grateful. What kind of rehab is it?"

"Detective Hall will give you all the details and location once she speaks with them tomorrow morning. It's a place for juveniles with low-grade criminal activities; those with drug addictions and they also address anger issues. They are strict in that they can have no visitors within the first three months of their time there. It is a six-month rehabilitation. I should mention that it's a private facility and quite expensive. How do you think your wife will feel about that?"

"I'm all for it. Money is not an issue when it comes to my children. It sounds exactly what Ben needs and I am sure Jessica will agree. I can't thank you both enough for this."

"No need. We will be looking deeper into this case. In the meantime, your son will be getting help for his other problems."

"Please thank Detective Hall also. Will you let us know when it's set up and he is being moved?" *He already felt some of his shoulder tension leaving his body.*

"Yes."

Michael ran down the steps to his car in their lot. He could not feel any better than he did at that moment. His first thought was to run in and tell his son the good news. Yet, he knew that would be unacceptable. The detectives would have to do that.

Happy for the first time in weeks, he traveled back up toward his home in Bucks County, his mind on Ben finally getting the right help. *Driving always seemed tedious to him. Yet today, he felt as if a blessing came upon them.* He hit one of the channels for classical music which always lifted his joy. *"Nothing can pull my spirits down today."*

— 100 —

As he hummed to the music, he glanced in his rear-view mirror and that black car with darkened windows that had been following him was speeding up behind him again. Once he closed in and Michael heard his motor become louder, he stepped on the gas to get away from the vehicle. That was when tragedy struck.

****

At that same moment in Cape May, New Jersey, Dana and her family were talking about the party they had been planning for this evening to send off their friends, Jake Stone, his wife Carolyn and son Scott to Texas. Jake had been a lieutenant in the Pennsylvania Pocono Mountain's police department for two decades. He had now been offered the Chief-of-Police position at the precinct in Texas. All who would be at the party valued the Stone family.

The surprise dinner party was to be at seven p.m. at the Lobster House on Landing Road. Dana chose the seafood restaurant in Cape May with a nice bar and a lot of atmosphere for the Stone family's going away party.

All the guests were to be there at six p.m., so as not to ruin the surprise. Dana and Nick expected their close friends and family, and their newest family members, Nicky and Michaela Pearson, along with Michael of course.

Dana was happy that Jake and his family would have a chance to meet Michael's second family before moving away.

After they all had lunch, they began wrapping Jake's gifts. Emily Rose had been fed and was content in her play-yard, giggling and humming. They had even purchased something for his wife and son. Nick was going to close the art gallery early for the occasion and be home by five p.m.

After the gifts were piled up on the table with lots of wrapping scattered around, Dana's phone lit up. "Hello."

"Is this Dana Campanella?"

"It is. Who is this please?"

"Is Michael Pearson your brother?"

"He is . . ." Her eyes wild looking, she turned toward her friend and shrugged her shoulders. "Is he okay?" Dana hit the speakerphone so Kate could listen.

"I am one of the nurses here at the Bucks County, PA hospital. I am sorry to give you this news, but Michael Pearson had your phone number in his wallet as next-of-kin. Your brother was in an accident and we need permission to do surgery."

Kate put her arm around Dana's shoulder.

"He's alive, right?"

"At this moment he is in critical condition."

"Of course, I give my permission. We will be there as soon as possible. Thank you." She dropped her phone on the table and sat for a minute.

Kate looked up the address of the hospital and put it in Dana's phone.

Her voice trembling, Dana asked her friend, "Would you mind staying here and contacting everyone that the party has to be cancelled?"

"Nick will probably want to go to the hospital when he hears, so I will also tend to Emily Rose." Her little dog Terry lay by their side.

"You are dear to us. Are you sure, Kate?"

"I am. Now go. Talk to your mom and get on the road."

CHAPTER SEVENTEEN

Bucks County, PA

After changing her clothes and kissing her daughter on the nose, Dana went into the kitchen to tell her mom the bad news.

"I'd like to prepare you for this shock, but there's not enough time. I must get to the hospital in Bucks County as quickly as possible. Michael has been in an accident."

"Not my son!" Louisa pulled off her apron and ran through the house to the stairs.

"Mom, where are you going?"

"Upstairs to change. I'm going with you."

While she waited for her mom, Dana called Jessica to let her know about Michael. Jessica promised that she and Becky would leave right away and meet them at the hospital.

The traffic wasn't too bad since it was a Sunday afternoon. When they arrived at the Newfound Hospital in Bucks County, Pennsylvania, she parked her car and they rushed in through the heavy front doors. A woman behind the front desk in the lobby asked if she could help them.

"We were notified that my brother, Michael Pearson, was in a bad accident and is in surgery here."

"Take this elevator up to the fourth floor, make a left when you get off and you will see a large waiting room. Someone will come out to speak with you after Mr. Pearson is out of surgery."

They followed her directions and made it up to the waiting room. There were not many visitors in the room.

While they waited, Dana thought about Michael's other family. She felt they should be notified but wondered how to do that with Jessica on her way to the hospital. She had automatically called her since she was still Michael's wife. She could not call Nicky until after Jessica left the hospital. Dana did not want to cause any problems for her brother.

"I don't even know if Jessica is aware of Michael's other family yet, Mom."

"Why are you worrying about that right now?"

"'I'm trying to figure out how to alert Nicky as to what has happened, but Jessica is on her way to the hospital now."

Before Louisa could respond, the double doors from the surgery area opened and a man in scrubs came toward them. The women stood arm-in-arm.

"Mrs. Campanella?"

"Yes." Dana extended her hand. "Please call me Dana, and this is my mother, Louisa Donato."

He shook both their hands. "Doctor Jason Swift. I am sorry about your loved one's accident. Why don't we move to this room? I'll close the door for privacy."

They followed the doctor to a nearby office with windows. He closed the blinds on the side of the room facing the waiting room.

Sitting across from the women, he began, "Michael Pearson is presently unconscious. He did get through the long surgery better than expected. He had internal bleeding and we had to remove his spleen, which will cause no harm. He also has a few cracked ribs on the left, as well as a broken leg—now casted. Most importantly, I'm afraid Mr. Pearson has suffered a concussion, which is the cause of his loss of consciousness. That will take time to heal. However, we expect he will have a full recovery. Do you have any questions?"

Louisa spoke first, "Do you think he is in a lot of pain, Doctor?"

"He shouldn't be. The nurses in the CCU will be out to talk with you about any concerns and give you visitation times throughout Mr. Pearson's stay in the unit. They address the pain and will keep him comfortable. Once Mr. Pearson improves, we can move him to a private room."

"Thank you, Doctor." Dana turned her head when she heard a knock at the door. "It's my husband."

The doctor rose and opened the door for him. "Dr. Jason Swift. Good to meet you, Mr. Campanella." They shook hands. "Have a seat. He turned toward the women. "I'll get that nurse for you now and she will also take you in to see your brother for a brief visit."

"Thank you again, Doctor." Louisa grinned at him.

"We will take good care of your son." He lightly touched Louisa's shoulder. With that, he turned away and went back through the double doors.

Dana was filling Nick in on Michael's injuries when his phone buzzed.

"Answer it. I'll get us coffees to go. Come with me, Mom."

"Hello, Detective Mason." Nick walked out into the hallway to hear better.

"Sorry to bother you in the middle of the day, but we need to ask you and Dana questions about your relationship with Britt McKenzie. Could you find time to come to the precinct?"

Nick hesitated at first, thinking it might be too much for Dana, then decided she would want to get it over with also. "

"How about six p.m.? We are at the hospital in Bucks County for my brother-in-law, Michael. His car was slammed by another driver on the road, and he went over an embankment."

"I'm sorry to hear that. Is he alert?"

"Afraid not. He is in critical condition. We are hoping that will change, as the doctors expect."

"Considering what you are going through, this can wait."

"No, we'll do it tonight. We aren't sure what will happen next in this situation. I am sure Dana will agree. See you then, Detective."

"Okay, thanks Nick." The connection ended just in time for Dana's return with two mugs of hot coffee.

While they waited to see Michael, he told her about their appointment with the Philadelphia Detectives.

The nurse came out through the double doors a few minutes later and took them into the CCU to see Michael. When Dana looked at him for the first time since the accident, she almost had to look away. It was a horrific sight. He was hooked up to so many things and had marks all over his face and neck. His head was bandaged and his leg in a cast. His usual ruddy complexion was as white as new snow.

When Dana stood next to his bed, tears formed in her eyes. Michael could barely lift his eyelids, but he did so when Dana spoke to him. "Michael, it's me, your sister. Your mom is here and so is Nick. We love you, Brother."

They all spoke to him, even though they received no response or movement. Dana held one of his hands, but it was limp. Louisa didn't come close to the bed. She was too distraught and anxious. The nurse came in within five minute's time. They took one last look at Michael and left.

Jessica and Becky were waiting when they came out from the CCU.

"How is he?" Jessica asked. Becky already had tears streaming down her face, and she didn't even see her dad yet.

"Honestly, you need to prepare yourself. He looks bad but be assured he will pull through this the doctor told us. He is going to need a lot of care once he leaves the hospital. Right now, he is still unconscious. It might take time to heal because, besides the other damages to his body, he has a concussion."

"It sounds like my dad needs a lot of prayers."

Dana hugged Becky. "Your dad is going to make it, Sweetie. But I'm sure prayers will be helpful."

"Thanks for being here. We'll talk later. I want to go in and see my husband now." Jessica hugged the two women, then took her daughter's arm and walked toward the double doors.

Once Dana and her family were in the car for the few hour drive back to Philadelphia, she made the call to Nicky. "Hi, it's Dana, Michael's sister."

"Hello. Michael has a lot of wonderful things to say about you and your family. I can't wait to meet you all. It's nice of you to contact me, Dana."

"Sad to say, this is not a social call. I wish it were. Michael was in a hit-and-run accident today. He's in critical condition."

"Oh, no! How bad is it?"

"He had to have surgery. The nurses will be treating him for pain after. He has a cast on one leg; and he has a concussion. He is unconscious right now."

Nicky gasped.

"We were assured today that he would eventually awaken. So, Michael is in the Critical Care Unit they call the CCU and you will get maybe a five minute visit with him each time you go. We have to go by their visitation times for the patient's sake. We were told he will be moved to a private room as soon as he becomes conscious and is healing."

"I have to see him now. Do you think that's possible?"

"Of course. Are you familiar with the Newfound Hospital?"

"Yes. It's not far from here."

"That is where Michael is in the CCU. I would advise you to only visit when Jessica is not there. I know Michael did not have time to tell her yet about you and Michaela. She just left the hospital a few minutes ago, so try to get in there tonight. Starting tomorrow, I will contact you as to when she'll be there, and you can plan your time accordingly. I am sorry, Nicky."

"I can't believe Michael is going through yet another crisis." She blew her nose and coughed a few times. "The police in our county need to get more officers out looking for this criminal. What are they doing, Dana?"

She felt Nicky's fear and pain run through her body. "The Detectives in Philadelphia are still trying to find Britt McKenzie's killer, and now they and the detectives in your precinct, specifically Detective Gentry, has his men out there looking for the road stalker who keeps harming Michael. Between the two cases, my guess is that they don't have enough manpower to get out in the streets. But what I do know is that if anyone can make my brother smile, it's you and Michaela, Nicky."

"I'd better finish getting dressed. Thanks so much for thinking of us. Michael is lucky to have such a wonderful sister. Talk to you tomorrow."

CHAPTER EIGHTEEN

Philadelphia, PA

Once Nick pulled away from the Bucks County Hospital, they headed toward Philadelphia to meet up with the detectives, as promised. It was only five p.m. with enough time for a bite to eat before going to the precinct. Halfway there, they stopped at a fast-food place. They ordered chips and dips. Then over coffee discussed what the detectives might want to ask them.

Louisa just listened while she drank her coffee.

"They already know we met Britt when we took her to the prison. And we barely know Ben."

"You never told me you went to a prison, Dana." Louisa's nose and forehead wrinkled up as she waited for an explanation. "Whatever for?"

"There was so much happening at that time, Mom. We didn't want you to have more grief after burying daddy."

"Okay, we can discuss that later. But you know I won't forget to bring it up at another time. Don't keep me in the dark. Instead of taking me to the police station with you, while you meet with the detectives, why don't you drop me off at Tony and Paul's house? I haven't seen them in a long time."

"Sure, we can do that." Nick was all for seeing his brother and sister-in-law again. "In fact, we haven't seen them since we returned from Paris. I think we could all use a visit." He paid for their food and they were back on the road.

Once they dropped Dana's mom off at his brother's home, they drove the few blocks to the police station. When the couple walked through the front door, Detective Hall was waiting for them at the front desk.

"It's good to see you. Thanks for keeping this appointment. It's important that we speak with you about the deceased since you seem to have been the closest to her. Follow me."

Dana allowed a sigh of relief to escape when they passed the room that held only bad memories for them. They were taken to a brighter and more comfortable room.

Detective Mason came through the door and greeted them. "We are sorry to hear about Michael's accident. Does he have any idea who hit him?"

As they sat next to one another across from the detectives, Dana answered, "Not to my knowledge. We won't know much more until my brother is conscious. The doctors fully expect that will happen soon."

"As we all know, Michael has been through a lot." Detective Hall placed the recorder in the center of the long table. "I can't imagine yet another heartache for your family."

"We are hoping he will be conscious tomorrow, and we'll be able to tell the Bucks County detectives more about the accident."

Nick was getting restless with the small talk. "Why did you have to meet with us? We are ready to answer any questions you may have." *Although he liked the detectives, he had too many bad memories at this precinct in the past and almost felt smothered just being there.*

"We won't keep you long."

Detective Mason began the questioning. "We know your family is now related to Michael and his family. It's understood that it hasn't been that long since you were all together. Tell us how well you know Michael's son, Ben Pearson."

Dana spoke up. "The first time we met Ben was in our home for a Halloween party last year, and again during the Christmas holidays before we left for Paris.

We felt it was the opportune time to get to know one another as a family."

"Can you remember back to those holidays and tell us how Ben acted around the other teenagers there?"

Dana again spoke up, "I suppose like any other child. I didn't pay close attention to each individual. There were no significant issues."

It was Nick's turn to speak, "We are not certain if Ben is just shy or has social issues with strangers. There were a lot of people at our parties as well. He may not have felt comfortable, and I noted he kept to himself."

"This may come across as very personal, but we would like to ask you about your trip to Paris," Detective Hall looked over at Nick.

"Sure, we had a lovely time." Once again Dana saved her husband from having to make something up to satisfy the detective. *She hoped the detective would keep the next question for her. She noticed her husband's one eye twitching and an air of disgust from his face. Patience is not one of his great virtues.*

"That's wonderful," Detective Hall sat forward. "Did you get the portrait finished in time for your buyers?"

"Yes. They loved it. It was a lot of work and trying to keep up with Victor Moreau's work schedule caused lost time for painting. But we did enjoy the breaks to see more of Paris. They are lovely people."

"Everyone needs a vacation like that." Detective Hall chuckled.

Detective Mason picked up the questioning, "You stayed in Paris from mid-January until your return in March. Is that correct?"

"Yes." Nick rolled his eyes over toward his wife. *Dana knew he was thinking--'let's get out of here now.' He didn't like to be grilled.*

"During all that time in Paris, did either of you return to the United States . . . for instance to your home in Cape May?"

"May I ask what that has to do with Ben?" *Nick wasn't sure where he was going with this line of questioning.*

"When we are working on a possible homicide case, we request the whereabouts of all who knew the deceased," Detective Hall stated.

"Did either of you return for business . . . a doctor's appointment, to check on your home, or for any number of reasons?" Detective Mason asked. "We would like to have the date and time if you did return." While silence ensued, the detective studied the couple.

Nick gave a quick glance to his wife. "I returned home to Cape May once for business. I stayed overnight and got a flight right back to Paris the next day.

The date was March twenty-ninth. I arrived back in Paris right before midnight.

Detective Mason kept the questioning up, "Thank you. Did you go anywhere besides your home or business in Cape May during those two days?"

"No, I did not leave our home until I drove to the airport the second day."

After scribbling a note on his desk pad, Detective Mason looked up at Dana.

"I never left Paris. My mother and Emily Rose were with us. The day Nick had to leave for business, my mom took care of Emily Rose while I worked on the portrait at the Moreau's home. My husband returned to Paris late the next day."

Detective Mason stood and put his hand out to him. "Sorry we kept you so long. Enjoy your evening. I hope Michael is awake when you return to the hospital tomorrow."

"Thanks." Nick turned to his wife who was shaking hands, then they followed Detective Hall out to the front desk. "We appreciate your time. Have a safe drive home."

They reached his car. He turned it around and headed for his brother's house with the local grocery store underneath. He had sold it to Tony before he and Dana moved away from Philadelphia.

When they arrived at the house and parked in the store lot, Dana looked over at Nick. "What do you suppose was the real reason Detective Mason grilled you on your whereabouts during our time in Paris?"

He shrugged his shoulders, got out of the car and held Dana's door open. "Beats me. I guess, like he stated, they have to ask those questions. Let's get inside. I'm anxious to see my brother and Paula."

Tony Campanella opened the door, "Hey Bro, give me a hug! You too cutie-pie." He hugged Dana. 'Bear hugs' were Tony's way of telling others he loved them. Paula came into the room and they got another big hug.

They followed the couple into the dining room to where Louisa was sipping her coffee. Their German Shepherd, Max, was happy to see them also.

"Have you been working out at the gym?" Dana asked Paula after that bear hug she gave them.

"I sure have, Honey. Thanks for noticing. You know I'm always trying to keep my weight down. I have a big appetite, so this is how I decided to take care of it." She turned her short, but now average size body for her height around for all to view.

Nick whistled, and Tony told them, "I can't take my eyes off her. We had to get a larger bed for some hanky-panky." He laughed.

"Okay, enough of that," Louisa told him with a titter.

"We missed you two while we were away. You always keep us smiling." Dana picked up the cup of coffee in front of her. "How did you know we needed this right now?"

"I don't associate with non-coffee drinkers." Paula winked.

"Plus, you have a long ride home when you leave here, so drink up and tell us what's happening with Michael." Tony pulled his chair in close.

Nick shook his head. "He's in a Critical Care Unit and in bad shape. The concussion he got from the accident caused him to become unconscious, so he is unable to speak right now. He has a cast on his leg and damaged ribs on one side."

"They have no idea who has been stalking him all this time?" Tony asked.

"No." Dana passed the creamer to Paula. "What's amazing is that this guy has been following my brother and running into the back of his car off and on for many months and they can't catch him."

"We are going to go up and see him tomorrow night. Right Paula?"

"You bet!"

"I'm sure he'll appreciate the visit, Bro—that's if he is awake by then."

They talked about Paris for a while, then Dana suggested they get going. "Kate has Emily Rose at the bed and breakfast with her and Austin. I don't know what we'd do without them."

Paula became sentimental. "It's nice to have people who love you and care what happens to you. I'm happy to be in our family."

"Me too." Dana hugged her. Tony joined in and pulled Nick into the hug before reaching for Louisa. "We didn't forget you." Max even jumped up and down around them.

After a lot of laughter, the three of them waved from the car before pulling away.

"Your brother is hysterical." Louisa laid her head back on the headrest. "He always keeps us joyful no matter how bad a situation might be."

"It's been a long day," Nick reached over for Dana's hand.

"I agree. There are parts of it I'd like to forget." She dropped her head back and closed her eyes.

CHAPTER NINETEEN

Bucks County, PA

Tony and Paula closed their shop on Sunday and made the trip to see Michael at the New-found Hospital. They got there really early in the hopes they would also run into Dana and Louisa.

The front desk sent them up in the elevator to Michael's floor.

A nurse walking through the CCU waiting room asked if she could help them.

Tony answered, "We are here to visit my brother-in-law, Michael Pearson. I believe he is in the CCU."

"Certainly. Let me check and make sure no one else is visiting right now. I'll be right back. Why don't you have a seat?"

"This is a lovely hospital. There are so many beautiful paintings on the walls and flowers everywhere," Paula pointed out to her husband.

"Yeh, they are nice."

"You seem nervous." Paula felt his forehead.

"What does my head have to do with being nervous? I'm okay. You know I'm not comfortable in hospitals."

"You'll get through it. I'm right here with you. We have to see Michael."

The nurse returned. "Okay, come with me and I will lead you in to visit Mr. Pearson. You will have about ten minutes at the most right now until he is able to have longer visits."

"That's fine. We are just happy to be here." Paula felt anxious too but didn't want Tony to know.

When they got into the room, Tony gasped rather loud when he saw all the tubes and other attachments around Michael in various places.

Paula sat in a chair right next to Michael's bed. He mumbled something she was not able to understand. "We are so happy to see you, my friend. We are sorry you have to go through this. Everyone sends their love of course."

Michael tried to talk, but he had difficulty. "Do you need something?"

Tony saw a plastic glass with a straw in it. "Maybe he's thirsty, Paula. Why don't you pour some of that water into the cup on his side table?"

"Good idea." She filled his cup halfway and held the straw while he sipped the water.

One of the nurses came into the room shortly after. "It's time for Mr. Pearson to rest. I hope you had a good visit." Paula looked over at Michael.

He tried to smile. She held his hand. "I know you will be having more visitors today. We don't want to wear you out. But we will be back to see you soon." Again, he almost smiled. It was more like a grin.

"Take care of yourself, Buddy." Tony followed his wife out to the waiting room.

"Hi there." Kate rushed over to hug Paula. Austin shook Tony's hand. "This is terrible. Dana's family has been through so much. Now after finally uniting with her only sibling, this happens." Kate had her hands on her cheeks.

Paula handed her a tissue, then put her arm around Kate's shoulder. "I am sorry, Honey. I know you are part of the family and have been for most of your life."

"Is he able to talk yet?" Austin asked.

Paula responded, "Not quite. He appears to make an effort, but nothing comes out. I feel like he is mentally alert by the way he moved his eyes when we spoke to him."

"That's a good start then. Dana told us the doctor feels he will make it, but it would take time for healing."

"Okay big guy. Let's get out of here before they throw us out." Paula handed Tony's jacket to him. She hugged the young couple. "See you both later."

It was Kate and Austin's turn to visit for the short ten or fifteen minutes allowed in the CCU.

CHAPTER TWENTY

Bucks County, PA

Dana and Louisa returned to the Newfound Hospital while Nick took care of Emily Rose at home. They had received a call around nine a.m. that Michael was conscious.

The hospital had also called Jessica since they had her number on file now. When they arrived, Louisa and her daughter were told that Jessica and Becky had gone in to see Michael a few minutes before them.

Dana and her mother took a seat among a few others in the waiting room, all hoping for good news. When Jessica and Becky returned to the waiting area a few minutes later, Dana and Louisa stood to greet them. They all hugged as Jessica was dabbing tears from her eyes. "Michael is awake, but he is having difficulty speaking," she told them. "The nurse claims his speech will improve gradually as his concussion continues to heal."

"I'm sorry. I can't believe this happened to him. Becky, how are you holding up, Dear?" Louisa placed her arm around the young woman's thin shoulders.

"I'm terrified for my dad and angry that anyone would treat him like this. He is such a good guy. Who would do this to him and why can't the police do something?"

"It's my understanding that the Bucks County Police are looking into it. They have labeled it a hit-and-run due to the fact that the other car slammed into Michael's to push him off the embankment. Then the stalker left the scene and never reported it," Dana explained. "Of course, the suspect took off. Michael's car was demolished from that and went flying down over the embankment, landing front first. Broken glass from the dashboard window was all over the place. Michael had been thrown onto a bed of large rocks nearby. It's a miracle he's alive after that kind of damage."

Jessica's mouth dropped. "Did he have a seat-belt on?"

"My guess would be not with that kind of destruction."

"Where did you get that information?"

"Our friend, Jake. You know he's in law enforcement."

"I hope they catch that crazy person and arrest him or her." Jessica pulled her daughter close to her. "We better leave now so you can go in and see Michael." They hugged once more.

"Safe trip home." Dana then checked the time and made a note of it to see if this was the time each day that Jessica would be visiting Michael.

"Same to you." Becky forced a smile.

Dana took a deep breath as they headed for Michael's room. Louisa looked at her watch. They were told they would only have ten minutes with him. At first, she hesitated to move close to the bed. She stared in disbelief at the tubes going into her son. She continued to stand in the doorway while Dana went over and took Michael's hand. He opened his eyes and peered into hers.

"Michael, thank God you are recovering. I am so sad this happened to you. Mom is here also."

He just starred at her but had no words. To her surprise, he squeezed her hand.

"I love you," she kissed him on the cheek. "As soon as you are moved from this unit, we will take turns being here every day until you are well."

He tried to speak. Dana thought he was trying to say thank you. Then his eyes left her, and he looked straight ahead.

"Mom, come over and sit here next to your son."

Louisa walked slowly toward the bed as tears trickled down her cheeks. She sat on a chair close to him as his eyes followed her. "My son, I love you. My heart is heavy for you right now. I pray you are not in great pain."

Michael very slowly moved his bandaged head slightly toward Louisa as a single tear slid from his one eye.

Dana spoke then, trying to get them both out of that mood. "We are glad Jessica and Becky were here to see you. I thought you might want me to contact Nicky and Michaela. I am sure they are waiting for you to return home."

Michael lightly squeezed Dana's hand.

She smiled at him. "I'll take that as a yes. I will call them. I'll try to coordinate when Jessica will be here and let Nicky know . . . at least until you get to tell Jessica later about your other family."

A nurse entered the room, "I am sorry, but your visit time is up. Mr. Pearson needs to rest now."

"Thank you."

She turned to Michael one more time. "Don't worry, I will get them here, brother."

"I love you, Son." Louisa kissed his forehead before they left the room.

Once they were out in the car, Dana quickly dialed Nicky's number. "Hi, it's Dana. I wanted you to know about a half-hour ago, Jessica and Becky left from visiting Michael. It's clear if you want to see him this afternoon."

"Thank you again for calling me. We will get ready to leave now."

"He's doing much better. He can't speak, although he is conscious and aware. Michael squeezed my hand twice to acknowledge what I was saying. That's progress. Enjoy your visit. Give Michaela our love too."

"Love to you also from both of us.

When they got into her car, Dana dropped the phone into her purse and pulled away from the hospital. *As she drove toward Cape May, she wondered if Michael had ever told Nicky about his deceased brother, Matthew in all the years they have been together. Or did he keep all that from her?*

CHAPTER TWENTY-ONE

Philadelphia, PA

When the Philadelphia Police van pulled up in front of the Jersey Shore rehabilitation center, Jessica Pearson was parked in front of them. She was anxious to see Ben and his surroundings for his six-month duration at the facility. *It was quite a distance from their home, but nothing would stop her from being there for her son.*

"Mom, what are you doing here?" Ben's shoulders dropped and his eyes rolled up in disgust as he got out of the police van."

"Well, hello. I am happy to see you too. I am here to sign some papers, but mainly to check the place out so we know you are in a good environment. Let's go in and see where you will be staying." She walked beside him, mindful of the two police officers behind them. They walked up about twelve steps to the front door of the beautiful building all in white stone. One of the officers held the door open for them. Once inside, the other officer signed some paperwork the front desk had for them. Then they wished Ben good luck and left the building.

The woman behind the desk made a call to someone, telling them that Ben Pearson was here and ready for his tour of the private facility. Within minutes, a young man arrived to greet him.

"I'll see you before I leave, Son."

"Could you please take this packet and have a seat to fill out some information for us, Mrs. Pearson?"

"Of course." She walked across the room and sat in front of one of the windows where the sun was shining inside and across the marble floor. It took her about twenty-five minutes to answer all their questions in the paperwork the woman at the desk had given her.

"Here you are. Jessica sat the papers down in front of the receptionist."

"Perfect timing." The receptionist was grateful. "Rodney will take you down the hall to meet some of the professionals who will help your son adjust while he is here. Then he'll give you a tour of the facility before you meet with your son again later. Enjoy your day."

"Thank you." She followed the young gentleman down the hall to a large room where many of those who would be working with her son were having breakfast. She met the team: counselors, nurses, social workers, and Ben's psychologist.

"We have a psychiatrist who works with the patients. He will be contacting you to chat over the phone since he is not here today," the social worker told her. Jessica was assured Ben would be in good hands during his time in the rehabilitation center. They had answered all of her questions, and she was reminded that there would be no visitation after this for a three-month period, at which time Ben would then be able to have visitors from his family during the last three months.

Jessica glanced back at the group as she stood to leave. "Thank you for caring for our son. They waved to her as Rodney led her to another area in the building. He took her for a tour. There were three floors, each with many rooms. She was taken to a large room with a library that held rows and rows, floor to ceiling of all kinds of books. Comfortable chairs were in a circle, and she noted a set-up of coffee and cups were along one wall. Small tables and chairs filled the other side of the room.

"That's a beautiful fireplace. I would imagine this is a good place for your patients to relax."

"Yes, Rodney confirmed. They spend time reading in here, or they can take a book to their room after signing it out."

Next, they arrived in the private living area, where each patient had their own small bathroom with the necessities in it. The room off from it had a single light and there were two lamps in the room, along with a single bed and a small desk and chair. He could look out at the lovely grounds outside the large window facing him while working at his desk.

"Down this hallway, we have a few meeting rooms. That's where we all gather in groups to give our patients time to speak what's on their minds. The meetings are held twice a week. The rest of the time, Ben will be working with other experts in their field on a one-on-one basis." A few of the other patients passed them in the hallway throughout the time they were there.

"It sounds encouraging. I didn't expect a rehabilitation center for addictions to be comfortable and attractive. I feel much better about leaving my son here. I am grateful for what you and your staff do for these young people."

"It's our goal to get our patients well. Similar to how we like to dress when we want to make an impression on people. We want your son and others here to care about themselves again by not relapsing when they leave here."

"We have a lovely dining area which you can view in the packet of information you were given. We also have a complete gym where our patients can stay strong and get rid of some of their frustrations." The staffer's phone buzzed.

"I'm told that Ben is ready to spend a little time with you and then see you off, Mrs. Pearson. He has been taking a tour as well and getting familiar with his room and meeting his team. Don't worry, we will take good care of your son."

"After this tour, I am not as worried. Thank you again, Rodney."

She was taken back to one of the empty meeting rooms where they brought Ben.

"Would you like coffee?" A gentleman in a white apron offered.

"No thank you. I had some earlier," Jessica replied. After he left, she touched Ben's hand across the table. "Honey, you are going to do well here."

He gave her an eye-roll and put his head down on his chest.

"Please try to cooperate. You will meet with professionals here who can help you get rid of your addictions. This is better than staying in jail, isn't it?"

"Yes, that's for sure. But I didn't kill Britt, so why am I being punished?"

"This is not a punishment. It's a blessing. They could have kept you longer at the jail for the drugs you carry around and share with others. That's an offense, and you also have a record with the department from a few months ago. You know you haven't been going to school or coming home much. You are sixteen, Ben. You need to get this treatment and try hard to stick with it. This place might change your life for the better if you give it a chance. That's what me and your dad want for you."

"Where is dear old dad?"

She froze, not having planned on Ben expecting an explanation of his dad's whereabouts. But she knew she could not tell him Michael was in a hospital all banged up.

"Dad is sorry he couldn't be here. You know he loves you, but he had to go to an emergency business meeting. It involves the funeral home, so he had no choice. I know he would rather have been here with you." *What a poor excuse. She felt bad her son didn't fall for it.*

"I guess that makes sense. It's way more important than me." He rose from his chair. "Maybe I'll see you again, Mom. Thanks for coming. I'm tired right now and want to go to my room and rest."

"Sure, Honey. You take care of yourself and relax. This will all work out for the best." She hugged him to her before he turned away and walked down the hall.

She thanked the receptionist and sat in her car for about three minutes while tears of joy rolled down her face as she tried to compose herself.

CHAPTER TWENTY-TWO

Bucks County, PA

A few weeks later, Meg visited with Michael at his home in Bucks County where he was recuperating. "I thought I would spend some time with you since Nicky and Michaela are out for a while."

"I'm glad to see you, Meg. How are things going with Laney and Charlie?"

"I don't know what I would do without a good friend like you, Michael. Even with all you have been through, you are kind enough to strengthen me to do what is needed in my life."

"We have been in one another's lives for many years, Meg. I have so many memories of the times you helped both myself and my brother. You were always there for us. I will be here for you. This is really a difficult move you will have today, but I think it's for the best, for you and for Laney and Charlie." He drew a deep breath. "I wish I didn't have this cast on and could be there with you for support. Remember you are doing this for the kids and their baby."

"That's what I will concentrate on . . . making sure they get the medical care they need, no matter what it costs me with my relationship with Laney."

"She might surprise you and not be as harsh as you are expecting. Either way, it's for the best for all of you. This secret has to come out now."

"I came to try and comfort you with what you are going through, and here you are, as always, making me stronger. I promise, I will do this, Michael. Do you need anything before I leave? Can I get you more coffee?"

"No, I've had enough for the day. The girls will be home any time now, so I'll be fine. Go and get this over with. We all love you, Meg."

"I love you too, friend."

She closed their front door and waited for the lock to go on before getting into her car to drive back to her condominium in Philadelphia, where she showered and dressed. She was getting ready for her promised visit to Charlie and Laney's home. Trying to calm her jumbled nerves, she kept talking to herself.

This was it—the day she could lose her precious daughter forever. Her plan was to start with the worst part then ease into the rest. After, she would tell them about the disorder of which they had to make their pediatrician aware. Laney would have to be checked also. Meg had looked it up and read it could be hereditary. She rarely had even a cocktail when she was alone, but before she left her home, she poured herself a glass of wine. It seemed to calm her enough to make the short drive to the kids home.

When she arrived at their condominium in the city, she parked at a meter instead of in the building garage like she usually did. *She figured she wouldn't be in there long, so why bother spending more than a dollar to park on the side street.* Trembling inside, she grabbed the folder next to her with medical information she had for the couple. Then on wobbly legs, she left the car and walked around the building to the front of the high-rise.

"Nice day." The doorman held the door for her.

She broke into tears and swiftly turned back out the door and ran to her car on the street. Drying her tears, she looked at the time. She had wasted another twenty minutes telling herself she could do this. She remembered how it was best for her daughter and their baby on the way. Thinking of her good friend, Michael, and all that he had to endure, she told herself she could do the right thing by her daughter and son-in-law. Using the rear-view mirror, she dabbed her tears away and fixed her make-up. She got out of the car, pushed her shoulders back and walked toward the building where the same doorman stood.

"Good to see you again, Mrs. Carson." He held the door open.

"Thank you so much." She smiled this time, then slowly walked through the lobby to the elevator, taking it to the eighteenth floor. When she exited, facing her was the couple's front door. Her stance now not so straight, tears once again filled her eyes as she paced the hallway. *She was re-thinking what she would say to her daughter and son-in-law. Maybe she should leave out Grace's disorder and tell them later. Picking one of her nails as she walked back and forth in the hallway, she knew that was not an option. She should have told Laney all of it when she found out the couple was having a baby. She stood still in front of their door.* "Oh, what a mess," she mumbled and the door in front of her opened.

Charlie stood in the doorway. "Meg, I thought I heard the elevator a few minutes ago. Come in, please." He held the door open. Choco ran over and licked her leg, then jumped up for a pat on the head.

"Mom, we almost gave up, thinking you changed your mind. Are you okay?" Laney hugged her. "Your face is flushed. Have a seat. I'll get you a cold glass of water." Meg looked over and smiled at her son-in-law, who she adored.

"How is everything?" he asked.

"Uh, well . . ." she hesitated to speak without Laney there. She wanted to get it over with at one time.

"I'll get you a glass of wine if you wish," Charlie offered.

"I would love that. Thanks."

"Sure." He left the room.

While they were both gone, she thought of how lucky her daughter was to have found a loving husband like Charlie. Dana and Nick did a great job raising him.

"Here you go." Laney handed her mother the glass of water. "It took me so long because the beef stew on the stove was bubbling over."

"Do you need help with it, Honey?"

"No. Relax and tell us what we have been waiting to hear since you left here when our friends had stopped by. Remember? Right before they got here, you mentioned there was something important you had to tell us. Let's have it." Laney got comfortable in a chair across form Meg.

"This wine is from the Vineyards in Napa Valle." Charlie handed Meg a glass. "I went into our stash downstairs. It took forever to find the one I wanted you to try, which is the wonderful *Chappellet Cabernet Sauvignon*. I think you'll like it."

She tasted it. "Exquisite." She took a few more sips and looked away from them. *It seemed she could feel their breath held tightly inside of their chests—waiting to hear the news. When she looked up again, she realized it was her breath that had stalled because she would be breaking their hearts.*

"Now, what did you want to share with us, Mom?" Laney fidgeted in her chair again. Charlie sat in another chair next to her. They both faced Meg.

She took another sip of the wine, which was more like a gulp. "This is the toughest thing I have ever had to do in my life."

"Is it *that* bad?"

She caught Laney reaching for Charlie's hand.

"I have a lot to share with you." She guzzled the rest of her wine. "It may come as a shock, but I hope you will let me finish before you respond." She watched them as Charlie put his arm around his wife. She also noticed the tight grip of their hands intertwined. But then Charlie stood and took Meg's wine glass. "I'll get you a refill. Would you like anything else?"

"No, that's fine." *She needed all the wine they offered.*

"I'll lay out some snacks." Laney turned toward the kitchen.

"That's not necessary," Meg yelled after her.

Alone again, she kept staring at the short distance to their door. *Every one of her brain cells told her to run while she had the chance.*

"We can nibble on these while we talk." Laney placed a dish of fruit, crackers and cheese on the table between them.

"That looks lovely," Meg managed to say. She was aware she had made them both nervous too at this point. She had to blurt it all out when Charlie returned—if only her heart would slow down a bit. *As an occasional cocktail drinker at events, she knew she'd need way more wine to get this secret out today.*

CHAPTER TWENTY-THREE

Philadelphia, PA

"Here Meg." Charlie handed her another full glass of wine.

The couple sat together again. "We're ready if you are, Mom." Laney and Charlie gave her a big smile. *She could feel the cracks in her heart.*

She finished gulping down the other half of her glass of wine before telling her tale. "I had a best-friend. We were three-years-young. She lived in the same neighborhood as our family. We became close from that time on into adulthood. We went to the same schools, and through college together. We shared a dorm the whole four years. The year we both turned twenty-one, we moved out of our parents' homes and started our adult lives. We each had bought a little house in Cape May, New Jersey. We were never far from one another even then.

Laney touched the heart area of her chest. "That sounds lovely."

"I notice that you keep talking in the past about your friend," Charlie stated. "Does that mean you are no longer friends, if you don't mind me asking?"

Meg took another swig of wine before replying. "You are right. We are no longer together. I am getting to that now. Is it hot in here?" She wiped her wet brow with a tissue from her bag.

Charlie jumped up and put the air-conditioner on, even though it was cold outside.

"That feels better already."

"What was her name?" Laney asked.

"Her name was Grace. She was the kindest soul I have ever met. We did everything together, including vacations. Life was good." Meg lowered her head for a moment then lifted it to speak. "Unfortunately, my best friend died in childbirth."

Laney's hand went to her mouth.

"How old was she then?" Charlie asked.

"We were both in our twenties. A few months before her child's birth, Grace became ill. She was in and out of the hospital numerous times before they finally diagnosed her with Cardiomyopathy."

"What is that?" Laney asked.

"A disorder that somehow affects a muscle in the heart. It causes problems with the heart pumping blood throughout one's body." *She left out the heart failure information.* "For my friend, it was too much. Grace died one week after giving birth."

Meg took another swig of the wine before her next words. "Once she had become ill and the doctors diagnosed her problem, she asked me to raise her baby as my own if she died. She begged me until I finally agreed. Then she swore me to secrecy."

"Why?" Charlie asked.

"Wait." Laney sat forward in her chair, dropping her husband's hand.

"Where is that child, and why don't I remember her, Mom? She would have had to be born around the same time as me. Right?"

Meg became so distraught at this point, she thought she would be sick. "Do you mind if I use the bathroom?" She didn't wait for an answer. She rushed out of the room and vomited as quietly as possible into the empty trash can. With shaky hands, she quickly cleaned it out. Tears poured from her eyes as she paced the bathroom in a square—grateful it was a large one. Fifteen minutes later, she returned to the den.

The couple stood. "Are you ill?" Laney sat a cup of hot coffee on the table in front of Meg's chair. She noted they had taken away the rest of the wine. The feel of her head spinning was a sign she had too much to drink. She knew she had to get this all out right now and take the consequences.

After a sip or two of coffee, she spoke slowly, "Grace was a loving person. She couldn't imagine her child growing up knowing that her mother died in childbirth. We weren't sure if she would make it through the birthing. Just in case, she forced me to swear to never tell you that you were not my biological daughter. She wanted her child to have a loving, normal life without any worries. That's a promise I made to her."

The silence was deafening. At first, Meg didn't know if those words came out of her mouth that loud or they were still silent in her mind. Every muscle in her body tensed, while waiting for her daughter to speak.

Charlie stared at his wife, who looked like she was in a shocked state. Even her eyes did not move when he spoke. "Honey, say something." Laney continued to stare at Meg in silence. Choco sat close to her feet.

"Laney, I love you with all my heart. I raised you from the moment you were delivered and put into my arms. I *am* your mother and always will be. Please forgive me for not telling you all this earlier. I was trying to keep my promise to my best friend, and to not cause you to have yet another problem along with delivering your son."

"Whoa, it just occurred to me that it means we were never siblings either." Charlie looked over at his wife. "Our baby should be born healthy, right?" He turned to Meg for that answer.

"We will need to discuss that further at a later time, Charlie. Right now, I am concerned about Laney. Can you say something, please?"

Her daughter stood, still glaring at Meg. She replied to her in a low voice

"Get out. Do not ever show your face in this house again. You are not my mother and never will be." With dry eyes and holding a hand on her large belly, she left the room with Choco following. They heard the master bedroom door close.

Charlie leaned over to hand Meg more tissues. "I am sorry. I get why you kept all this secret. But I think it will be a long time before I can get Laney to come around. It's all quite a jolt, don't you think?"

Meg wiped her tears away. "I should have let you both know earlier. The reason I am telling you now is not only to ease the pressure off you both believing you were siblings all this time. More importantly, you must read this medical information and share it with Laney's doctors. I did not note it in there, but this can be a hereditary disorder." She stopped to catch her breath for a second.

"Because it can be handed down through families, after Glen is born, he will have to be checked as well. I would not mention that to Laney until after she has the baby because that disorder is what killed her biological mother while giving birth." She handed him the folder. "Once the doctors know about it, they can check her heart *before* she gives birth. They will test her and know what to do. She has never been sick other than a cold. Please continue to take good care of her and my grandson. Of course, I will be there for all of you whenever Laney is ready to accept me in her life again."

With that, Meg stood, hugged her son-in-law and rushed out their door to the elevator. The doors opened and she stumbled into the empty square. Unable to control her shaking and tears, she allowed the elevator to drop to the floor below. Then she quickly pushed the button to stop it from moving and fell to the floor in a fetal position—wailing.

CHAPTER TWENTY-FOUR

Cape May, NJ

Dana, Kate, and Louisa came together to plan the party for the Stone Family. They were leaving for Texas in less than a week.

Dana's mind was on the kids and her new grand-baby. "I hope nothing interferes with us having this celebration." During breakfast she had called the restaurant to make sure they still had reservations for that evening. "It's all set up." She put her phone on the table.

"It's good we all agreed on sending them off from the restaurant. Having it at home is more fun. Yet, there's so much going on around us these days. I dare to draw my attention to all that work and time when we could get a call that we're needed by the kids."

The conversation went to Jake and his family and how much they would all miss them. Nick had spoken to him earlier. "They agreed to do their vacationing once a year in Cape May. Jake told me that Carolyn is all for it."

Nick was happy for their friend moving up in his career. "I wish them well. I expect Jake will be busy in a new precinct. I'm sure he'll do a great job though."

"I think he will. Enough coffee for me." Louisa got busy wrapping the gifts. "Our adorable Emily Rose will be up soon. I don't want to miss our play time."

They all arrived at the restaurant at five-fifteen p.m. to make sure everything was in place. They had ordered the decorations, and the restaurant was to place them in the room they were using for the party. The Stone's believed dinner was at seven-thirty p.m., which gave their guests plenty of time to arrive earlier.

Emily Rose wore a cute little pink and white polka dot outfit with ruffles around the bottom of her blouse. She had a bow to match in her curly mane. Emily pranced around her play-yard all smiles, clapping her hands and giggling.

The first to arrive were Paula and her husband. "Here's our gifts." Tony sat them on a side table where he noticed others put their packages. "Where is everyone?"

Dana laughed. "We are here, Tony. The Stones think dinner is for seven-thirty. That allows enough time for all the guests to arrive. In fact, it's really only our usual group. Charlie and Laney can't make it.

Michael is still laid up, but we'll get to meet Nicky and Michaela."

"Don't forget Meg will try to make it since Laney and Charlie won't be here," Louisa reminded them.

"That's wonderful. How is she making out with moving back to Cape May?" Kate asked

"She is here today to clean her little house off the bay she purchased. I hope you didn't forget that tomorrow we all help her move in and put her belongings away." Louisa couldn't imagine anyone forgot. She loved helping others move in their new homes. She was grateful too that they helped her and her husband when they had moved in with Nick and Dana."

"Sorry," Kate admitted. "I did forget, but I'll be there. Thanks for reminding me. I think I need a brain vacation these days."

Nick let out a whistle for everyone to listen up. "The place looks great and it's almost time for the guests' arrival. I'll turn the lights down."

They all refilled their cocktail glasses while they waited to get into position.

"How will we know they are here?" Louisa whispered.

Dana answered, "The restaurant has their names. When they come in and identify themselves, a buzzer goes off in this room. Only we can hear it. That alerts us to get into position."

"Wow, there are so many great gadgets in this world today." Her mom chuckled.

A second later the buzzer went off and they all hid in the darkest part of the room. When the lights went on, they yelled, "Congratulations, Jake!"

Hugs and laughter were everywhere after that. Dana was concerned that Michaela and Nicky had not yet arrived.

Jake's son, Scott, introduced a young man who came with them. "Meet my friend, Blake Elis." He looked to be around the same age as the boys. Everyone welcomed him. Scott burst out a wide smile.

By the time they all sat around the table that was large enough to accommodate them, Nicky and Michaela arrived. She apologized, "I am sorry we are late. The traffic was heavy."

Louisa greeted them. "We are happy you could make it, Ladies." After she took their coats, she pointed to the location of the women's restroom. Then she took them to the table and introduced them to everyone. "I would like to introduce Nicky Collins, Michael's significant other, and their daughter Michaela Pearson." She then hugged them both. "I am Dana and Michael's mother."

The others got up and welcomed the two loves of Michael's life.

Louisa picked up her granddaughter. "This is our sweet Emily Rose. She is our lovely lady."

"She is beautiful," Nicky took her little hand in hers.

Michaela leaned down to her level, "You look so pretty, Emily Rose."

Over dinner, they first discussed Jake's promotion to be the Chief of Police in Texas.

"We know you will make a great chief." They all clapped.

"I am honored to get this job, but I know the pressure will be much

higher than my work in the Pocono's Precinct."

"Honey, I think you'll do a bang-up job," his wife, Carolyn assured

him. "I'm lucky also to get a transfer to the medical field in Texas. The

work is similar, higher salary, and I'll finally have a secretary. The best part is that I won't have to be there late at night like in my old job in the Pocono's."

"That's wonderful. We know how much your lives were disrupted because of all the extra hours you had to spend on the job you had in the mountains. Sounds like you are both set to succeed." Nick agreed with his wife.

"What about you, Scott?" he asked. "Do they have any Veterinary colleges in the area where you will live?"

"They do," Scott answered. "It's only a few miles away from our community, and Blake is also studying to be a Veterinarian. He and his girlfriend already live in Texas. I'll be staying with them until I get my own place there."

"Nice." Kate put a 'thumbs up' at the boys.

Dinner finally arrived. Dana had ordered for all of them, letting them know ahead it would be a steak and salmon type meal. Of course, they could order any sides they wanted to go with it.

Nick had already purchased two bottles of champagne for the party and brought them with him.

After dinner, when dessert was served, they all picked up their glasses so he could make a toast, "May happiness and success stay with you, my friends, throughout your time in Texas and beyond. You will be in our thoughts and I hope on our beach every summer. To the Stones!" Glasses clinked.

They all returned to Dana and Nick's Victorian home after for coffee and cake, and to give Nicky and her daughter a tour.

The women went off by themselves to get to know Michael's family better, while the men sat around and talked more about Jake's move.

Upstairs, Charlie, who had come to the party himself for an hour to wish them good luck, was giving Blake a tour of their home. He seemed really interested

"Thanks." He turned toward Scott, "This is exactly what I think you will need when you look for a place to live in Texas." He laughed at his friend's shocked look.

"This house is way too big and expensive."

"I was just teasing you, Buddy."

"Yeh, I was considering something much smaller.

Blake changed the subject and turned to Charlie. "I'm sorry your wife and baby couldn't come with you. It would have been nice to meet them.

Charlie explained, "It's too soon for them to be out. I can't stay long. I want to get back and help Laney so she can get some rest. So, you are going to be a Veterinarian also. Have you always wanted to work in that field?"

"That's the plan, Charlie, and yes I have. I have four dogs at our home in Texas. They are my buddies," Blake confirmed.

"What are you doing under the bed, Charlie?

He was on the floor, looking for something. "When I arrived, I put your gift from me and Laney under the bed. It's small. I hope it wasn't vacuumed up. Oh, here it is," he reached further under his bureau.

He handed it to Scott as Blake looked on. "Open your gift."

When he opened it, both their eyes almost popped out. "This is Amazing!" Scott's eyes widened and his mouth formed a circle as he whistled.

Charlie had a big smile on his face. "We heard from the grapevine that you have a girlfriend. We thought this would be a good gift for you to have some fun together before beginning your career.

"Thanks, Buddy. You have been my best friend all these years." Scott hugged him.

"Impressive," Blake added

"I can't take the credit. It was Laney's idea. We thought you would be able to use a month's vacation in the Bahamas. Enjoy before you begin school out there."

"Charlie, everyone is leaving," Nick yelled up the stairs. "Are you coming down now?"

They took off downstairs. Charlie gave his good-byes right away. He had to leave. "I'm worried about Laney being home alone with the baby." He hugged his little sister, Emily Rose and kissed her head.

The hugs, kisses, and some tears spread around the room as Nick.

Dana walked the Stones down their long set of steps to their car. "We are going to surprise Michael before we drive home. I hope he's up to some visitors." He turned and faced Nicky. "What do you think? Would you and Michael mind if we stopped by your home to spend a few minutes with him and say our goodbyes?"

"I know he was upset about not being able to be here to see you off, so

I expect it would be wonderful for Michael to see you all before you leave.

Why don't you follow us?"

"No doubt he will love that, Jake. Safe trip and don't forget to call us when you get settled into your new digs in Texas." Nick tapped his shoulder.

Kate and Austin left also. Tony and Paula were the last to leave.

"You know, the store opens early every morning. Let's go, you old fart." Paula gave her husband a light punch in the belly. Then they hugged the family. "Thanks for including us. We'll see you soon." They left for Philadelphia.

CHAPTER TWENTY-FIVE

Cape May, NJ

M eg was in the process of returning to Cape May, New Jersey, her hometown. After two months of no return phone calls from Laney; her letters sent back to her unopened; and gifts she had sent for the baby returned to her, she felt it was time to give up the condominium to the kids and move out. It was also too heart-breaking for Meg to be only one mile away from her new grandson's home. Yet she was not able to see him or care for him while Laney and Charlie went to college daily and then work, as originally planned. Someone else would take care of Glen.

Glen Charles Campanella was born to Charlie and Laney. Dana had called to let her know. She was happy for Louisa Donato, who now had a great-grandchild since Charlie is her grandson, and Nick and Dana are grandparents. This makes Michael an uncle to two boys.

Kate and Austin were going to the hospital later towards evening. They are going to be Glen's Godparents.

When Dana had called Meg to give her the news of the birth, she told her that Michael is still laid up, but he contacted Charlie to congratulate them. He was happy to learn they are all well.

******

A few hours later, at the Philadelphia hospital, Dana, Nick, and Louisa entered Laney's room. The baby was in Charlie's arms. Dana got up close. "Look at my beautiful grandson! He is adorable. I love the red hair." She hugged her son and put a kiss on her daughter-in-law's forehead. "How are you feeling Laney?"

"I'm relieved that our son is finally here, and that neither of us has the disorder that killed my biological mother during childbirth."

"What disorder?" Louisa asked.

Charlie attempted to give it a name, "Cardiomyopathy. I was told it's a problem with one's heart muscle and can be hereditary also. I am happy Laney and Glen were cleared of it in their tests." He let out a loud sigh.

Charlie nudged his mom. "Don't you want to hold your grandson? I thought that would be the first thing you'd do." He laughed and handed Glen over to her.

"This little guy resembles you, Charlie. This gorgeous red hair must have come from his mama," Louisa teased as she hugged them both.

At first, Nick was speechless, just taking in his family's love for one another. It was finally his turn to hug his grandson. He was a bit nervous trying to get him in the right position in his arms. Charlie and Laney laughed with joy.

Next, it was great-grandma's turn. "You should have gotten Glen first, Louisa." Nick handed the baby over to her.

"What a good child. We haven't heard a cry since we entered the room." The baby opened his eyes slightly. "Oops, I hope he wasn't offended by my comment." They all laughed with Great-Grandma, Louisa.

A nurse came in and stated it was time for Glen's one other test they had to do that day. "We'll take good care of your son, mom and dad." The nurse left the room with their baby.

They all sat around the bed.

"They can come home tomorrow. We can't wait!" Charlie hugged his wife and kissed her on the cheek.

Nick stretched his arms. "We had better get going and let you rest. I believe Kate and Austin will be here soon, and I'm sure Tony and Paula will drop by as well. Did you hear from Michael?"

"Yes. We know he is still healing from his injuries. He wished us well and wants to get together soon." Charlie was looking forward to seeing his uncle again.

Everyone hugged the couple, then Charlie walked them out to the elevator

"Thanks for coming by. My son is awesome, right?"

Nick gave him a high--five. "You, my son, are also awesome!"

Dana put her arm on Charlie's shoulder. "I'm proud of you both. You have a lovely little family. We are here for you anytime you need us. Don't forget that."

They got into the elevator and waved to Charlie as the doors closed.

CHAPTER TWENTY-SIX

Cape May, NJ

Meg's home in Cape May is situated near the new bookstore by the bay. It sits back away from crowds of people. Her friends offered to come and be a part of putting her house together. They have done this for one another every time one of them moved.

Dana and Nick arrived first, since they live close by in Cape May. "I love it." They checked out the house. "This beauty is made just for you. How many bedrooms?"

"Two, one bath, but as you can see, I have a large kitchen and a small patio in back right off the bay."

Dana hugged her. "It's perfect. Should you have an overnight guest, there's the other bedroom."

"I do love it. I missed Cape May while I lived in Philadelphia. Yet, I stayed for my daughter and Charlie. I feel lost without them now."

"I know you will always feel that way until Laney comes around. Give her time. You made the right choice for yourself. We are always here for you."

"Thanks, Dana. It means a lot to me." She turned as the front door opened.

"Wow, this is a cute little home. So cozy," Kate squealed as she and Austin entered. They hugged and sat around the kitchen table with Dana and Nick. "Where is Emily Rose?"

"We put her down in the bedroom for a nap. She didn't sleep well last night. I'm sure she'll be awake as soon as she hears all of us out here."

They had finished off two pots of coffee by the time Tony and Paula arrived from Philadelphia.

"Glad you could make it," Nick gave his brother a bear hug and kissed his sister-in-law's cheek.

Tony greeted them all, then asked, "Where's that adorable baby of yours?"

"She is taking a nap, but I'm sure she'll be up shortly."

"I have her while you all do the heavy lifting." With that, they heard Emily crying in the other room.

"Keep working, I will get the little lady and even change her diaper." Tony went toward the bedroom and the crying stopped.

They all heard him say, "Come to Uncle Tony, Love. You are too cute to be in bed this time of day."

He lifted her up and gave her raspberries on her belly. She giggled. They went into the living room and of course everyone fussed over her. Then Paula suggested he put Emily Rose in her play-yard.

Tony picked up the baby from the floor and sat her on his lap. "She's too smart to be put into a cage."

Paula corrected her husband, "It's not a cage. Play-yards are popular now because they give the child more space to move around."

"If you say so, but she wants to play with me." He sat Emily on his knee while the others helped Meg pull the house together. Louisa always headed for the kitchen first. Kate and Austin unpacked boxes and placed the items where they looked good or served some purpose.

Paula cleaned the bathroom. Meg put her bedroom together as Nick brought in the items for that room.

Dana had warned everyone ahead of time to not bring up Laney or the baby. *She wanted this to be a happy day for Meg. She cared about both women and felt that Meg should have shared her secret earlier with Laney. Yet, she wasn't willing to wreck their friendship by voicing her opinion, especially when they were now family. Dana held a lot of empathy for those she loved and was happy her friend returned to Cape May.*

Once all of Meg's beautiful art, china, and various other pieces for her new home all had a special place, she pulled the lasagna out from the oven. She also had salad in the refrigerator, and Louisa helped her set up the counter for all the food. She had beer and juices on the counter also. "Dig in everyone. Thank you so much for helping me move all these things into my new digs. You are wonderful, as always."

Dana picked up her glass of water, which led others to do the same. "A toast to the beginning of an exciting life in Cape May, New Jersey for Meg."

They all clinked, then got in line to fill their plates before they followed her out to her little deck facing the bay. She had a large round table and chairs out there she had purchased when she first checked out the house. She decided it was just what she needed when the weather cooperated.

All agreed the food was delicious. They were now onto coffee to wake them up before they had to drive home. Dusk was upon them. Tony and Paula had the longest ride back to Philadelphia.

"Has anyone spoken to or visited Michael lately?" Kate asked.

Dana spoke up. "He is getting around the house well with the crutches. I know he is bored and can't wait to get back to work."

"He still has the cast on his leg." Austin added.

Louisa chimed in, "I believe he told us they will be removing it in a few weeks."

She was also thrilled to meet Nicky and Michaela. "They are both so sweet and beautiful. I am glad they made it to the Stone's party. It gave all of us an opportunity to get to know them better."

Kate came in from the kitchen. "I didn't get to talk to them much at the restaurant. We need more time with them. What does Nicky do for a living?"

Dana told them she is highly educated. "Nicky is a professor of science and biology at their local Corbet University in Bucks County."

Tony chuckled. "Really? I'm impressed. I was lucky to graduate eighth grade in my day."

"Okay, family, let's clean this mess up now and leave Meg to get some rest. It's getting late." Louisa took the dishes out to the dishwasher. Dana and Meg followed. Nick and Tony stayed on the deck to chat.

"I think this little one is ready for bed," Kate hugged Emily Rose to her one more time. "I'll get her changed and ready if you'd like, Dana."

"That would be great. Thanks."

By the time everyone was leaving Emily Rose was asleep in her daddy's arms. Meg's home looked lovely and comfortable. She thanked all her friends and wished them a safe ride home. Locking up, she took a shower, dressed in her pajamas and climbed into bed. She felt tired, but as always happened when the silence arrived, her mind was on her daughter, Laney. She began her nightly prayers of asking for her forgiveness to come soon.

CHAPTER TWENTY-SEVEN

Cape May, NJ

In the little Café where Dana and her friends loved to meet, she shared with Kate the situation in which Meg found herself recently. "I invited her to have lunch with us, like old times. I feel so terrible for her. She knows she should have shared her secret with Laney much earlier, but she was afraid of losing her—which is exactly what happened when she finally told the couple that she was not her biological mother."

Kate put her coffee cup down. "What? I cannot believe that. How could she not tell Laney that years ago when she felt she was old enough to understand?"

"It's not that easy to risk losing one's child when she or he finds out you and/or your spouse are not their real parents. Plus, reality is that Matthew was an animal and not living with them most of the time."

A shudder traveled through Dana's body at the mention of his name.

"Then Meg adopted Laney?"

Dana ended up telling her the whole story. Meg had told Dana ahead of time it was okay if Kate knew.

"It sounds like the good of it is that Charlie and Laney are not siblings like we thought. Matthew wasn't her real father, right?"

"No, thank goodness. Meg told us Grace, her best friend, never mentioned who Laney's father was or how it happened. They never spoke of him, so Meg didn't ask. Even though this takes the pressure off Laney and Charlie that they could have healthy children, Meg paid the price." She shook her head from side-to-side.

"This is one of the saddest stories I have ever heard, next to yours. Laney won't talk to her at all?"

"It's been a few months. Meg called her with no response. She had written her letters, and sent gifts for the baby that were returned, so she has finally given up for now. The kids had paid for the condo where she lived, with the inheritance money Matthew left Laney. They wanted Meg to live nearby in Philadelphia to help take care of Glen when he was born. They both have college during the day and work from home a few nights a week. Meg knows her daughter well, and she does not expect her to accept her forgiveness for a long time, if ever. She chose to give them the condominium back by returning to Cape May to live. She can only hope that one day, Laney will realize how much she loves her mom. This is the only other place she has good memories with Laney, and I am glad she is here with us."

"What are her plans?"

"She needs to find some kind of work to keep her busy."

"Doesn't she write and illustrate children's books?"

"Yes, for years now. It seems she only works on them a few hours a day and will need more for a decent income."

Kate's eyes lit up with excitement. "I have a temporary job for her if she wants it. Austin and I are going on a trip for a month to an island. There wasn't much time for a long honeymoon after the wedding in January. You know Meg well. Do you think she would be interested in taking over the Bed & Breakfast until we return? It might even cheer her up."

"What a wonderful idea. I can't wait until she arrives. It will keep her mind busy."

Just as Kate began telling Dana about her trip, Meg entered the café. Dana motioned to her.

"Hi! I'm so glad I can join you. You were all such a great help in putting my house together."

Dana touched her hand. "You never have to thank us."

"I am sorry about what happened between you and Laney. I am sorry to also hear she will not respond to you. I believe she will reconsider when she realizes how you gave her your whole life to raise her into the beautiful woman she is today."

"Thanks, Kate. It's sweet of you to say that, but I'm not counting on it anytime soon. We should talk about something else."

"We have a lot to discuss after we order. Kate has a great offer for you. I don't think you will turn it down," Dana teased.

"Sounds exciting."

The waiter arrived at their table. "What can I get you ladies?"

Dana ordered a grilled cheese and tomato sandwich. Meg chose tuna on rye bread and a side of coleslaw. Kate asked for a meatball sandwich, with sauce and coleslaw.

While they waited for their food, Kate spoke up. "Austin and I are going on vacation next week. We need someone to take over our *Comfy Bed & Breakfast*. I was going to ask Louisa who is familiar with handling the B & B, but I remembered that you need a job, Meg. While we were waiting for you, it occurred to us you might be the perfect person. What do you think?"

"I'm shocked. I cannot believe I'm being offered a job so soon. I expected to be looking for quite some time."

"We will be away for a few weeks. I can show you what you will be doing, how to handle new vacationers, and where everything is located. You have full use of our personal living quarters on the first floor. It's all attached yet sectioned off from the rest of the Bed & Breakfast by a solid door."

"It sounds wonderful and challenging. I love people, so that part should be easy. Thank you so much, Kate. I accept your offer." She went around the table and hugged her. "You sure made my day!"

"I am grateful to you for accepting the job. I know you well, and I won't have to worry about a stranger taking over while we are gone."

"Where are you going?"

"The Bahamas—where else?"

"That's wonderful. I am envious though."

Once they were finished more small talk and their coffee, Dana suggested, "Let's check out the new bookstore down the path."

Dana peeked in through the store front. "It looks like someone is in there. Maybe he'll give us a tour of the shop. Nick will be thrilled to learn about this place. He is obsessed with books. We are going to have to add on another library in our home soon."

When they hit the bell, a gentleman held the door open in greeting. "Hello, Ladies. Jackson Hunter." He offered his hand.

"We had lunch at the café and thought we would stop by for a little tour of your bookstore if that's okay. Are you open for business now?"

"I am. Feel free to walk around. I'll answer any questions you have. You are officially the first customers to enter this bookstore."

"I see you have a lot of children's books." Dana found one for Emily Rose while the others were chatting. Hearing part of their conversation, she told Jackson, "If you need any help in that department, our friend here, Meg Carson, is a writer and illustrator of children's books."

"That's good to know. How long have you been in that business?"

"About five years. I work on them part-time at home."

"Look at the time. I must get back before Austin. I promised him a super dinner tonight."

"I'd like to check this book out, then we can go." Dana handed the book to Jackson. "It's for Emily Rose who loves having stories read to her."

"You can purchase it, or you could go the return method."

"I'm collecting books for my little daughter, so I will purchase it, thank you. It's great that you have another option though."

"This is a lovely bookstore. We wish you well, Mr. Hunter." Meg thought he was really helpful. She was sure to return soon.

"Please, call me Jackson. Once again, thank you for your interest and come back soon." He walked them to the door, held it open, and waved as they walked away.

"I'll bet Jackson Hunter will be calling you to take a job at his bookstore, Meg." Dana looked over to get her reaction before leaving them.

Meg's mouth dropped open, and her eyes enlarged. "If only!"

CHAPTER TWENTY-EIGHT

Bucks County, PA

Home and getting used to walking on his leg without the cast, Michael tapped the number for the Detectives handling Ben's case.

"Hi, Detective Mason. Michael here. I'd like to give you information I withheld when questioned at your precinct."

"Good to hear from you. It sounds like you are on the mend."

"I am and grateful for it. My daughter and I plan to visit Ben at the rehabilitation center soon. Thank you again. I wish I could have been there when he was moved."

"Does your precinct know yet who did this to you?"

"They are still trying to figure it out. As you know, stalkers are difficult to weed out from the general population. I suppose I'll keep looking behind me when I can drive again."

"Let's hope they catch this criminal before that. So, what's on your mind?"

"I know my son is innocent. He may have anger issues and drug problems right now, but it's all my fault. We thought our children bought the pretend happy marriage we presented when they were home. But I believe that is what brought on my son's breaking point."

"I'm sorry to hear about your marriage not working, but do you believe that you affected Ben enough for him to go into a rage and kill Britt McKenzie?"

"Ben has anger issues toward me, but he would never kill or harm anyone. What might have prompted him to go to Britt's condo is this: I have a second house here in Bucks County. It was right before Ben went to Britt's apartment that he discovered this house. He and his friend, Josh hid in the bushes. Later I found out the boys had followed me here from the funeral home." Michael stopped talking to take a sip of water. "More importantly, Britt McKenzie stopped by here at the same time the boys were hiding in the trees that surround my property. I believe when Britt left and I walked her to the car, he saw her kiss me on the cheek. I'm sure she didn't mean anything by it. Yet, he must have taken it the wrong way and went to her apartment to let her know it was not acceptable to him. That doesn't make Ben a murderer."

Detective Hall agreed. "Why didn't you tell us this when we questioned you, and how did you know it was Ben and this other kid in your bushes?"

When Britt left the driveway and headed for the road, she had to stop suddenly because a car came by and it was Ben and Josh. She called me right away and told me they had probably been the ones we heard running through the bushes. She was positive it was Ben. I had planned to tell you all this when I got home, but never made it. It was the day of my accident." *Michael knew in his heart that his son was not guilty of Britt's death.*

"Okay, Michael. Let me check into this further, and I'll get back to you."

After Detective Mason broke their connection, he turned to his partner. "It looks like you could be right after all, Carla."

"About what?" She was studying their board, hoping they had not missed something.

"You tried to convince me that Ben is innocent. Keep that thought." He picked up his coffee thermos and headed for the door. "I want to try and find more witnesses on that street. If Jim Cash saw something, there has to be other witnesses who were afraid to come forward."

Carla grabbed her coffee mug. "Wait. This project is finished. I'll come with you."

When they reached the street where Britt's crime had taken place, Detective Mason got a call from their precinct. "What's up?"

"There's a guy on the other end of this line who claims he has information about a crime that occurred on Walrush Street recently."

"Does he live in the area?"

"He didn't offer any other information, but he did say he has photos."

The detective sat forward in his seat. "Put him through." With raised eyebrows, Detective Mason looked over at his partner and put his phone on speaker.

"Hello, Detective Mason."

"This is Jamison Bentley. Stay with me now because this is a very odd situation. There's a camera shop on Walrush Street, not far from your precinct. I have a business in Center City, Philadelphia, and I took my Canoke into that shop to have it repaired. When I picked it up to test it out, I took a panoramic video of the buildings across the street. I then viewed one or two shots to make sure it was working well. I had my active four-year-old grandson with me."

With frowns, the detectives looked over at one-another. Carla yawned, and Brock put his feet up on the desk.

"The camera was still videoing when I had to grab my grandson from running into the street. I had not used my camera again until my grandson's birthday party this afternoon."

"I assume by this information you are giving us, you picked up something on the camera that would interest us, Mr. Bentley?" Brock let out a sigh.

"I'm sorry I made a story out of this. Yes, after taking photos at the party today, my daughter and I viewed them and were surprised to see a woman laying across her terrace rail at one of the condominiums on that street."

They both sat up and listened now. "That's on your camera? Do you have other footage?"

"I do. Right now, I am leaving here to go home. I can stop by for you to check it out."

"Definitely! Can I have your business address, Mr. Bentley?"

"I'm at 207 Center Street in the city."

"Ask for Detective Mason when you arrive here. Thank you for reporting this."

"Okay. See you in about thirty-five minutes."

Brock disconnected the call and turned to Carla. "What are the chances of something like this happening? It has to be Britt McKenzie in that photo shot."

"I sure hope so. What would help Ben's case more is if there's a correct time on Bentley's camera."

They got out of the car and returned to their office in the police station.

"Can you make a new pot of coffee and put it in the room we are using, while I go to the lady's room, Brock?"

"You make it so much better, Carla. You know I always put too much coffee."

His partner frowned at him, then laughed. "Put less this time." She left the office.

They had a room set-up down the hall, coffee and water ready, and were still waiting an hour later. Carla looked over at her partner. "Can you please stop tapping your pen on the table? I have never witnessed you so anxious. What's going on?"

"This is big! If this guy has what we need, Ben is free from being a suspect, and we can be out there looking for the real killer."

"He didn't say there was a killer. If his camera only shows her leaning over the terrace, she could have done that herself. If the time on his camera is accurate, it should tell us whether it is a homicide or suicide, Brock."

"Why can't you be optimistic . . . at least in this case?"

CHAPTER TWENTY-NINE

Philadelphia, PA

J amison Bentley finally arrived at the police
station. An officer up front led him to the
room where the detectives were waiting. "Sorry
I'm late."

"It's okay. Thanks for coming in, Mr. Bentley." They
all shook hands.

Detective Mason placed the recorder in the middle of the table. "Have a seat."

"Would you like coffee? It's freshly brewed," Detective Hall offered.

"Thank you. I have been rushing all day. I could
use it."

She went to the small counter in the room and
poured him a cup. She returned to the table and they
waited until he took a few sips.

"You do have your camera with you?" Detective
Mason asked.

"Oh, yes." Mr. Bentley took his rather large camera out of its bag and handed it to Detective Mason, who sat it on the table between them. "You don't mind if we record our conversation, do you?"

"No, go right ahead."

"Can you repeat what you told me on the phone earlier? We know your grandson distracted you from the camera, and therefore you have shots you didn't plan on taking. What exactly did you see in the film that alerted you and your daughter?"

"As I explained to you over the phone, there's a woman leaning over the metal rail of her terrace. Having heard about the death of a woman going over her terrace in that location, I thought I should share this."

"Did you see her land on the ground?"

"No, I must have shut the camera off, unknowingly. Maybe they were practicing for a play or something?"

"The detectives glanced at one another with a look of surprise. Detective Mason looked over at him, "You used the word 'they.' Can we assume there was someone else in the photo as well?"

Detective Hall sat forward, "Did he or she push the woman, or watch it happen from the same terrace?"

"I don't know if he was watching her, but there was a very tall man in back of her. He was facing sideways when the shot was taken. I believe he was then looking away from the woman. I could not see his entire face. The photo is not clear. We saw nothing else after that except for our family shots. I am sorry it's a short section in the camera."

"Don't worry. We appreciate you bringing this to our attention," Detective Hall assured him.

"Would you mind if we kept your camera overnight, Mr. Bentley? We are only interested in the photos that might show a crime scene. It will not leave our precinct. We have experts here who will pull our photo up and examine just those shots in which we are interested and enlarge them for us. It might help our case."

"I have no problem with that. Give me a call as to when I can pick up my camera."

"That's not necessary. I know you are a busy man. We will have one of our men return it to you first thing tomorrow morning. Will you be at your office then?" Detective Hall asked.

"I usually arrive at eight a.m. every day. Here's my business card. I hope you find what you are looking for but be prepared. I believe that scene with that woman is real."

"Okay, we will see you tomorrow. Thanks again."

"I'll walk you out, Mr. Bentley." She held the door for him.

As soon as they left the room, Detective Mason turned off the recorder. He grabbed his coffee, the camera, and took off to the second floor of their building to their digital imaging experts.

"This is urgent," he told Janson, one of their top guys in the field. "We need everything enlarged, close up, and as detailed as possible. There could be a man in the background of a woman flying off her terrace. We need the surroundings, and any other scenes that relate and can be viewed clearly. Don't touch the other personal takes of the gentleman's private shots. What we are looking for should come up toward the beginning of the video and probably only cover a short space. We have to return this camera by tomorrow morning." He stood. "I'll be at the pub. Call me as soon as you have something." He ran into his partner in the elevator. "Let's get dinner."

"Did they say how long this might take?"

"No, and I didn't ask. I don't want to rush them and have them miss something. They know they have until tomorrow morning. But you know our guys. We'll get a call tonight. Let's go. I built up an appetite now."

"Something new?" Detective Hall teased.

"What do you think about this, Carla?" They talked as he drove the three blocks to their destination.

"It could be the break we've been hoping for in Ben's case."

Brock looked over at his partner. "Yeh, the kid certainly is not a tall guy, which is how Bentley described the figure behind the woman."

"If our guys can get a good shot of this male, the next step would be checking to see if he has a record."

"They parked outside the local pub and ordered as soon as they got a table.

"I'll have a small pizza with mushrooms," Brock told the waiter when he arrived at their table. "Oh, and a large coke."

"I would like a tuna steak and a house salad. Coffee will be fine."

"You have to show me up, don't you?"

"What are you talking about, Brock?"

"Can't you break down and for once eat a hamburger and fries, instead of that healthy junk?"

"I am waiting for you to do the same before you're back at the doctors again for your blood pressure."

"Yak . . . yak . . .yak! Let's change the subject."

Carla laughed.

"It's times like this I feel like you are my wife."

"Hold that tongue! Neither one of us is marriage material with the job we have here."

"I don't know. I'm a handsome guy. Lots of women like really tall men."

"Yep, it goes well with your ego."

"You don't deny you are a beautiful woman, do you? New officers coming in fall all over you. It's disgusting."

"It's like babysitting, Brock, and your charm is getting you nowhere right now."

"Get out of here. You love me. You wouldn't want any other partner." He grinned at her just as the waiter arrived.

The waiter sat their plates in front of them. "Thank goodness. Take a bite, Brock."

He had a few bites of his pizza, then got back into their discussion. "If our guys do come up with a clear photo of this suspect at Britt's apartment, do you think it might be the one she had been dating?"

"Could be. Maybe she threatened to tell his wife and he didn't want to risk that."

"Michael did say she was upset and couldn't let go of the thought of losing him."

"We need to check her phone calls ourselves, and any other communication she had with others about this guy."

Gulping down the rest of his soda, Brock pulled out his card, grabbed the bill and paid it on their way out the door. As they reached the car, his phone buzzed.

"Detective Mason. Yes! We are on our way."

Back at the precinct, they rushed into the elevator to the second floor.

"What do you have?" They pulled up chairs for themselves.

The detectives quickly studied the enlarged photo. "Wow! You got a great shot of this guy. How many men have a star tattoo on the side of their face? Do you recognize him, Carla?"

"No, how about you?"

"Same here. He looks unruly, unshaven, his shirt rumpled like he had to use some muscle to push the victim over the terrace. I'm sure she tried to fight him off."

"Or maybe he took her off-guard and she thought he was grabbing her for a hug and didn't suspect his plan to toss her over."

"Good point."

"Can you blow this up a bit larger and give us a few copies to post around the neighborhood? Also, did you get anything related to this case?"

"Not much. I think you are lucky to have gotten this shot. We got our artist to work on putting out a portrait of his face."

"That's a huge help. We'll take it. Good job." Detective Mason stood.

"Here's the camera owner's business card. He works a mile or so away. Can you get one of your guys to return it tomorrow morning after nine a.m.?"

"No problem."

"Thanks Buddy."

The detectives returned downstairs. In their office, Carla put the coffee on, and she began making space on their board for the photocopy that would come down to them soon.

"We have to get hold of forensics to see what other prints they had picked up the day of Britt's death. I remember them stating some were not a match for Ben, like the rest of the prints they had."

"We are fortunate to get such a vivid copy of this guy." They both stared at the enlarged photo on their board once it was brought into their office. Carla commented, "It would have helped more to have a full-face shot."

"Now, the tough work." Brock took the hot mug of coffee from his partner

"We need to find out who and where he is these days."

CHAPTER THIRTY

Philadelphia, PA

Detectives Mason and Hall left the precinct and drove over to Walrus Street. They had posters with them of the suspect's side face showing his tattoo. If they got no response when they knocked on doors, they rolled up the poster and stuck it in their mailbox. They both spoke with people they felt could have witnessed Britt's murder from their condominium terrace across the street. Only a few people opened their doors to them. They claimed they saw and heard nothing.

The detective asked, "Do you recognize this man?" Those who answered the door shook their heads no or stated that they were not home during the hours of the murder across from them. "We are getting nowhere. I think people are afraid to get involved. You know how that goes, Brock."

"I sure do, but we have to find this guy. Let's drop these posters off to our men who are placing them on the poles."

They dropped off their posters to those working for them who were a block away.

"Let's get back to the precinct and see if our guys upstairs have found anyone who resembles this guy in any way," Detective Mason suggested

"His half-face is not in our database. We have a lot of posters out there now, so hopefully someone will speak up soon."

The detectives went back to their office. They had just sat at their desks with coffee, ready to make a lot of phone calls to those they felt could help them out when the front desk buzzed them.

"Detective Hall."

"We have a gentleman here at the front desk by the name of Jerry Bennett who claims he knows the guy on our posters. In fact, he looks like him."

"Check him out for weapons, then bring him up here," Detective Hall ordered.

"What was that about?" Detective Mason ended a call that got them nowhere.

"There's a male downstairs who claims he knows the person on the posters and is here to give us information. Our officer says this guy looks like the poster.

There was a knock on the door. Detective Mason opened it to one of their police officers and the guy on their board. "Is he okay?

"He's clean." The officer left as the detectives stared this guy down for a few seconds, amazed that he came to them. He was clean-cut, very tall, and they spotted the tattoo right away.

"Have a seat, Mr. Bennett." Detective Hall placed the recorder in the middle of the table. "Okay go ahead and tell us your story."

"I live two blocks down and saw the posters when I came out of my house today. I thought it better to come in and let you know that I am not guilty of Britt McKenzie's murder. I know it looks suspicious that I was in her apartment that day, but I left her condo after we had a conversation, and she was very much alive as I drove away."

"What was your relationship with Ms. McKenzie?" Detective Mason asked.

"We had a short affair, maybe over a period of six months. Britt did not take it well when I ended it. I'm married and told her at that point that I would never leave my wife."

"Does your wife know about this affair?"

"She does now because Britt called my home when I was not there. She told my wife about our relationship."

"So, you came here to do what, if you didn't kill her?" Detective Hall asked.

"I went to her place for the last time to plead with her to let this go and move on. My wife was upset. In time I believe she will forgive me. I wanted to impress on Britt that I would never see her again."

"How did you do that, Mr. Bennett?" Detective Mason asked. "By pushing her over the terrace? That photo we have of you shows you standing in the background."

"Yes. I was turning toward the stairs to leave, which I did while Britt was still leaning over the rail. She didn't seem suicidal or anything, so I left the building. What is strange is that when I went down the stairs and out the front door, I noticed a man across the street standing in front of a condominium. He was staring up at Britt's terrace. As I walked to my car, I noted he quickly went across the street right to Britt's condo. The front door must have still been unlocked because he got right inside. I figured she was expecting him since she was all dressed up, and I went about my day."

"What did this guy look like?" Detective Hall asked.

"Short, maybe five-foot-five or six. He had a lot of dark hair, was stocky, maybe in his late 40's, and I noted he had some kind of limp. I didn't see his face directly except from across the street."

"What time would you say you noticed this guy?"

"I had an appointment, so I did check the time and left there at four forty-two pm."

"Ms. McKenzie was still leaning over the terrace?"

"Yes."

"Do you think you could give a description of this guy to our artist?"

"I can try. Like I told you, I didn't see his face up close. But I think I could describe what I did see I suppose."

The detectives took him upstairs and watched as he and the artist worked together. In the end, they had enough of a portrait to have their people post the photo around the neighborhood.

Back downstairs, they took information from Jerry Bennett, his phone number, address, license number, and a photo for their board. They were not totally ruling him out as a suspect, but they made sure he wouldn't take off either. "Do not leave this state without our knowledge, Mr. Bennett," Detective Mason told him. "You are still a suspect."

"I understand. I don't usually leave the city since my work is here. I will check back with you if I have any further information."

"I'll walk you out," Detective Hall offered. When she returned to their office, Brock put his phone down. "I called his home to see if he gave us the right address. His wife answered. She told me he wasn't home."

"What did you say to her?"

"No problem. I'll call again."

Carla pushed a number on their business phone for the coroner. "Hi Luke, can you give me Britt McKenzie's time-of-death? I just want to double check it."

"Sure, it was 4:45 p.m. Anything else?"

"Not right now. Thanks."

"Good move, Carla. That is definitely after the time Mr. Bennett claims he left Britt's condominium at 4:42 p.m."

"That means if this guy is telling us the truth, the male he saw going into Britt's place right after him could mean we finally have her killer."

"Let's hope someone recognizes this suspect."

CHAPTER THIRTY-ONE

Bucks County, PA

Michael rose early from sleep to help Nicky prepare for Becky's visit for that afternoon. He adored his family, and he hoped they would all have a good relationship with one another. He knew it would be a long time before he could include his son.

"There you are." Nicky sat on the bed beside him. "Stop thinking and let's have a wonderful day." She hugged him. They kissed, and then she helped him up.

"I'm happy that cast is off," he had a grin on his face.

"It will be a relief when you can put more pressure on your foot in a few days. Breakfast in twenty minutes, my love."

Michael pulled her over for another quick kiss, then closed the bathroom door behind him.

By the time he got down to breakfast, Michaela was helping to set the table.

"Hi, Dad. How are you feeling?"

"Good, I'll feel super with a hug from you."

Michaela laughed and leaned in under his strong arms.

"Are you excited to meet with your sister today?"

"Half-sister, right?"

"Sure. You won't have to always address Becky as such. We all know you have different mothers. It's okay to refer to one another as 'my sister' don't you agree?"

"It's okay with me. I'm happy to have a sibling. It gets lonely at times when I want to share my thoughts with someone closer to my age."

Nicky hugged her daughter on her way to shut off their stove. "That makes sense, Honey. Keep in mind that she is thirteen years older than you. But I get that you would feel more comfortable with that difference in age than ours for some conversations." She winked at their daughter.

Once breakfast was over, they put up the streamers in the front room that read: *Welcome Home, Becky. We love you*! with red hearts following.

"You both did an excellent job on this," Michael praised. "Although I'm not crazy about the glitter all over."

"Ok, Dad. I'll clean that up later."

"It's okay," Her mom assured her. "Leave that job for me tonight when you and your big sister will be getting to know one another. Becky's room is ready. After she is here awhile, and after the tour of the house and grounds, I think you should be the one to take her up and lead her into her bedroom, so she knows where it's located, Michaela."

"Thanks, Mom. That will be fun. I like that she's at my end of the hallway."

When Becky arrived, they all hugged and sat down with their coffee before getting Michaela's new sister settled in upstairs. "This is a beautiful home. I had no idea you had so many acres. It's amazing."

"As soon as you are ready, we will take you for a quick tour of the house and the grounds if you wish," Nicky told Becky. "I am not sure what time you have to leave for Ben's visit today."

"We planned to be there about three p.m. before they have their dinnertime. Why not freshen up. Then we will take you around before leaving for the rehabilitation center."

"Sounds good to me, Dad." Becky followed her new sister up the winding stairs, both holding luggage.

Nicky curled up next to Michael. "I'm sure the girls will get along. Michaela is glowing with even having someone she can call sister. I am excited for her."

"Yes. I think it's the best thing for both of them."

When the girls came down the stairs, they took Becky outside to view the grounds, swimming pool, outdoor/indoor patio, and the amazing number of trees that surrounded the area.

"Well, you have toured the outside of our home, now how about the inside, then we can leave for the rehabilitation center," Michael suggested.

"I already took her through our home while you and mom were outside."

"Great job, my dear Michaela. I suppose we should get on the road, Becky." He put his arms around Nicky and Michaela. "I wish you could both come as well. But I think it's too early to introduce you both into Ben's life with what he is still going through. I am sorry."

Nicky gave him a hug. "No need. We do understand why we have to wait to meet Ben. Now go and enjoy your son."

Michael kissed both of them and waved goodbye, although he felt sad in a way that he couldn't introduce them to his son today.

CHAPTER THIRTY-TWO

The Jersey Shore

Michael and Becky drove off to Ben's rehabilitation center for the first time. Over the phone they had been told that visitors were not accepted until three months were completed by their clients. Ben had two and a half months left before he would be released.

"I know you are as happy as I am to finally see your brother."

"I am, and thanks for having me overnight, Dad."

"You are always welcome. My home is yours too. We are all family now. In time Ben will meet Nicky and Michaela. I wish it could be soon, but it will be a slow process, giving him time to learn and accept all the changes made while he was gone."

"You told me the detectives feel this is the only way Ben might give up the drugs and alcohol. I feel the same way. He is in a good facility, not for just a week or two like some, but six months. That's a long time for anyone in Ben's position. Yet, the longer he is in there, the more chance it will change him." Becky glanced at her dad. "Don't you think so?"

"I do. Those in-and-out rehabs usually do nothing for people with these problems. Time is everything. Jessica is supposed to meet us here by noon. I don't see her car. Do you mind sitting here for a few minutes until she arrives, Becky?"

"That's fine with me. She's already been here to sign Ben in, so she knows how to get around the place." She turned in her seat to face her dad now that the engine was off. "Tell me more about Nicky and Michaela. You've been with them for a long time. What are your feelings?"

"I love them both so much. I think you will grow to feel the same. You are easy to love, Becky. I am sure they will enjoy every visit they have with you. I would like you to consider living with us. That killer is still on the loose. You can't stay in a hotel yourself. You do not want to stay at the funeral home without protection. It's not safe. Please consider my suggestion. We would love to have you with us."

"I will consider it and give you my answer by the time I leave tomorrow."

"Thank you."

Jessica arrived and parked behind them. They both got out of the car to greet her. She hugged Becky. "Hello Michael." She walked in front of him, not even looking into his face.

"Hello," Michael replied. Their relationship was restrained at that point in time. "Shall we go in now?" He held the front door of the rehabilitation center open for the women.

They went to the front desk to sign in where a young lady greeted them. "Hello, how can I help you today?"

"We are here to visit our son, Ben Pearson."

The receptionist pushed a number on the phone at her desk. "Ben Pearson's family is in the lobby." She then turned to the Pearson family. "Please have a seat and a tour guide will be here in a few moments."

As the three of them sat across from the front desk, only minutes had gone by when a gentleman appeared and led them to Ben.

They all hugged him. *Michael was so happy to see his son. He couldn't believe how good he looked and even had a smile on his face.* "I apologize for not being here when your mother signed you into this rehab. I am fine now, Son. But I had been in a bad car accident. I couldn't leave the hospital at that time."

"No way! Why didn't you tell me when you were here, Mom?"

"We didn't want to cause you any worries while you were working on your own problems, Honey."

"It's over now. I'm fine, and you look great, Ben. I just didn't want you to feel bad that I wasn't here for you until now. It looks like your time here has been good for you. We are grateful. Let's enjoy this day together."

Becky put her arm around her brother's shoulder. "Tell us what you have been doing."

"I have made new friends here. They have been here awhile and helped me realize that fighting being here didn't accomplish anything. We have meetings together, and then we meet with the professionals alone, like the psychiatrist, social worker, and many others."

Michael put his hand on his son's shoulder. "Sounds like you are well-cared for, Ben."

A gentleman came up behind them. "If you are ready, Mr. Pearson, I will walk you through the facility with your family."

Ben walked next to his sister. She put her arm around him. They were taken into all of the rooms in which Jessica had viewed when their son first arrived at the rehabilitation center. Michael and Becky were impressed with his room and bath, as well as the huge library and all the rooms they went through. They were even able to speak with the psychologist on Ben's case. He assured them their son was becoming familiar with the rehabilitation rules.

After the tour, they were taken back to the sitting room and served coffee, pretzels, juice, and yogurts.

Their guide smiled as they all took a seat. "Enjoy your time together. I will return in an hour to help you check out."

"Thank you." *Michael had been so anxious to see his son, he thought he would burst.*

"This place is amazing!" Becky was impressed with the rehabilitation center in which her brother now resided.

"Do you really feel they are helping you, Ben?"

"Sure, Dad. We have a lot of meetings, which at times can be boring. But I am learning a lot from others who have almost completed their time. One guy told me this rehab has a history of very few addicts returning here after their six months."

Jessica reached over to touch her son's hand. "I am so glad to hear that."

Michael was amazed at the new Ben, even with the short time he had spent there so far. He was able to talk about his experiences, and for the first time in a few years, was sociable and seemed to want to heal.

While enjoying their snacks and coffee, they all told Ben what was happening in their lives . . . being careful to not speak of any big changes that had transpired, or of the stalker.

Their hour was up, and the tour guide appeared. "I hope I have not returned too early."

Jessica thanked Rodney. "We are grateful to have had this time with our son."

Michael thanked him also. "We look forward to taking Ben home soon."

"Yes, Sir."

They hugged him. "I am so proud of you, Son." Michael was beaming as they watched him walk down the hall with the guide.

When they reached their cars, Michael turned to Becky, "This may be the best decision the detectives ever made for your brother. We must thank them."

"I agree." She kissed her dad's cheek.

His smile warmed her heart.

Becky waved goodbye to Jessica as they got into their cars.

When they were back at the house, they joined Nicky and Michaela. They were out in the back barbecuing dinner: chicken, salmon, hot dogs, and burgers all on the grill. Afterward, they sat around and chatted until they digested their meal. Then they all jumped into their in-ground pool nearby. Michaela was holding onto her dad's arm on their way into the house after they ended the day with roasting marshmallows. "I'm tired." Michaela bid all a good night, hugged her sister, then dragged herself upstairs to her room. Nicky made the three of them hot cocoa, which they drank while re-living the great weekend they had with Becky and their visit to Ben's rehabilitation center.

Becky put her head on her dad's shoulder. "I've had a wonderful time here with all of you. I feel blessed to have all three of you in my life." She stood and hugged her almost stepmom, and then her dad. "Thanks for a wonderful time. I have to go to bed before I collapse though."

Nicky laughed. "I'm with you, Becky."

"Hey, wait for me," Michael yelled as he finished his cocoa and took the stairs one at a time.

CHAPTER THIRTY-THREE

Bucks County, PA

The next day, Michael turned over in their bed and pulled Nicky to him before she could fall back to sleep. He glanced at the clock on their end table. "I can't believe the time. Did Becky leave for her vacation yet?" He got up quickly hoping to see her before she left.

Nicky laughed. "Take your time. I'm afraid she did. None of us wanted to wake you. She will call you later and wanted to thank you again for a wonderful visit."

"I take it Michaela left for her friend's house overnight. I should have been up early. It's been a busy two weeks since I got the cast off my leg and feel normal again. We haven't had much alone time. What do you say?" He ran his fingers through her silky black hair she recently had cut to her chin.

She snuggled up to him, kissing his face and neck. "Let's see what you got, big fella." She jumped up, laughed, and ran into the bathroom to turn on the shower. Michael followed and joined his lovely partner. They were believers in not wasting water.

Downstairs in the den a while later, they discussed eloping. "It's not important to have a big wedding, but it is my wish for us to be married soon. We have waited so long, as you have stated in the past."

"Are you sure? I thought all brides had to have their special day with a big party and tons of people around them. That's not you, Nicky?"

"What do you think?" She had her hands on her hips.

"I think we should elope. I will check with Becky and see that she doesn't set up any funerals for whatever Saturday you select next month. My divorce is final as of two weeks from today. Plan on, my love."

Nicky sat on his lap with her arms around his neck. "Thank you. I love you," she whispered in his ear. "I can't wait until we can tell Michaela. Of course, both daughters should be with us. Do you agree?"

"You have my vote. I wish Ben was able to help us celebrate. We couldn't get him even for one day. I want to be very careful how we deal with this whole situation when he is released from the rehab for good."

"I think that's the right thing to do . . . take it slow. We can wait until he is home if you think that will help him."

"No. I think the opposite. Introducing you to Ben as my wife might mean something more to him after he knows about the divorce with his mom."

"Whatever is good for your child works for me."

Michael stood up and headed for the kitchen. He brought back some wine and chips. He sat them both on the table in the family room in front of the fireplace. Just as he got comfortable, his phone buzzed. He looked over at Nicky, "I hope the girls are okay on their adventures. Hello." Listening to a voice on the other end—one he did not recognize, he suddenly sat up straight and placed his wine on the small table in front of them.

"Who is this?" Then he stood.

Nicky took his free hand as she caught the fear in his face.

"You'll do what? I'll call the police right now if you don't put Jessica on the phone." He managed to press the speaker so she could hear the man's voice.

"I'm afraid she is indisposed at this time."

"Michael, help me plea . . . !" *He knew it was her screaming, her voice shaky and full of fear.*

"You freak! Why are you doing this?"

"It's simple, my man." the scratchy voice on the other end of the phone did not sound familiar.

"Did you ever hear the cliché—An-eye-for-an-eye? Now, it's your turn to suffer. How does it feel, Michael?"

Before he could speak again, they both heard a gunshot. The phone went dead. Nicky screeched as she held tight to her future husband. He took her and his keys hanging on the front door, locked it up and led her to his car. Picking up his phone, he called the Philadelphia precinct as he drove. "Detective Mason or Hall. This is an emergency." As he waited for one of them to respond, he hugged her tightly to him.

"Detective Mason here.

"It's Michael Pearson. I need the police and ambulance to get to my apartment at the funeral home in Philly right away. I think Jessica has been shot. I'm driving there now, and Nicky is with me."

"How do you know she's been shot?

"A strange man called and had us on the phone. Then we heard a gunshot. Next, we heard Jessica's voice begging for help. Please hurry, detective. I'll meet them there."

"Wait, hold on, Michael. The emergency vehicles and ambulance are on their way. Detective Hall is heading there now too. The shot could have been fake just to get you there also. Can you tell me who you think was on the phone?"

"Don't know. I have never heard that voice before. I feel like he was muffled. He called me by name, so he must know me. Maybe he's the guy who has been stalking me on the road all this time. I feared leaving Nicky alone in case he knew about our house."

"Good move. I'm on my way now. By the time you get to your place in Philadelphia, Detective Hall will be waiting outside in a police car. Nicky will be safe with her while we go inside."

"Thanks. See you there." Michael squeezed her hand. "You heard that. Please stay with Detective Hall until we find out what is going on. I am so relieved that Michaela is at another sleepover today, and Becky wasn't at the apartment when this guy arrived. Thank God she changed her vacation plans to this weekend."

CHAPTER THIRTY-FOUR

Philadelphia, PA

Michael and Nicky drove the rest of the way in silence. *He felt as if he was going to vomit at any moment. His stomach rumbled. He hoped the detective was right—that this guy just wanted to scare her.*

When they pulled up inside the funeral home parking lot forty minutes later, it was filled with police cars and two ambulances. Detective Mason was outside the apartment door waiting for them.

Michael hugged Nicky, then watched as she got into Detective Hall's police car. He then rushed over to the building.

The detective pat him on the back. "It's best we stay here in the hallway until the paramedics bring Jessica out. We want every piece of evidence we can get from your apartment so we can put this criminal away."

"Oh, no!" Michael yelled. "It's true, isn't it?" He felt like he was losing his balance. He grabbed the frame of the wall and leaned against it. "She *was* shot!"

The detective put his arm under Michael's before he replied to him, "This guy assaulted her, so I want you to be prepared. Her face, neck, and arms are bad. She's in a comatose state . . . most likely due to the number of blows to her body and head; not to mention the level of pain she must have experienced."

"It's all my fault," he leaned against the brick wall for support, his head down and his hands covering his face.

The detective put his hand on Michael's shoulder in silence until a few minutes passed when he pulled himself together.

"Where was she shot?"

"Jessica was not shot. It appears the suspect shot the wall in the room once. This is more personal than just a gunshot wound. By the marks around her neck area, after he beat her, it looks like he tried to strangle her. We figure he heard the sirens when my men arrived, and it scared him off."

Michael tried to hold back the scream he wanted to release as he realized this guy intended to kill his ex-wife. But why, and who is he?

"Your officers saved her life. Otherwise, he would have finished her off, right?"

"It looks that way. As you know, Michael, we must investigate further before I can comment on anything else. The next building over is very close to yours. Yet, it sits much higher. Any number of residents could have looked over if they heard the gunshot and witnessed something happening inside your apartment or saw him escaping. Let's hope there's one or more witnesses here. Police are in that building next door right now, questioning residents. Forensics is in your building getting as much evidence as they can find. We will get this maniac."

They waited for the paramedics to bring the victim out. "I'm sorry this happened to Jessica, but there is no love lost between us."

Detective Mason changed the subject. "Based on the fact that you feel it could be the stalker on the road, he might have also been the hit-and-run driver who almost killed you, and now he chose Jessica to get your attention. We need to put all man-power we have on this with us in Philadelphia and the detectives in Bucks County." The detective stopped talking and moved something in his ear

"I'm told the paramedics should be out any moment. Let's discuss this later. I know you are both shook up. If you are planning to see Jessica at the hospital, you can stop by the precinct before you go home. It's a rough time, but the sooner we can catch this dangerous offender, the less chance he tries to kill you or one of your family members again. We won't talk long. Any information you might have that we are missing will be a plus."

"Okay, we can do that."

They could hear the men bringing the stretcher down the stairs inside the hall. "You will only be able to observe her for a second. I know how much you've been through, but they have to get her to the hospital right away. By the way, where are your children?"

The detective was interrupted by the appearance of the men carrying the stretcher.

"Fellas, can you hold on and give her husband a second?"

The two men stopped abruptly, gently put the stretcher down, and stood aside.

When Michael viewed his ex-wife's face and head so swollen that she was unrecognizable, he vomited on the side wall. The detective handed him some tissues.

With tears in his eyes, Michael nodded to the detective and stood still as the stretcher passed him. *That's when he noticed, at the end of the gurney, an officer carrying a see-through bag with a pair of bright red shoes—identical to the pair that Britt McKenzie had on when she met her death. Michael dropped into the hallway chair, trying to pull his mind together as to what they might mean to the case. Jessica had only been around Britt twice at Dana and*

Nick's home in Cape May. It wasn't as if they were friends who would go shopping together and select the same shoes. He had never seen Jessica wear that type of shoes in all the years he had been with her.

Detective Mason had gone inside for a few minutes and just returned. "Your complexion has suddenly turned pale."

"Whew!" Michael wiped his forehead and eyes with his shirt—a move he had never done before. *He was known for being meticulous because of his business.*

"I apologize for falling apart. The whole scene is surreal." Michael stopped talking when he heard the sirens as the ambulance pulled away. *He couldn't believe a human being hated him enough to harm those close to him. He was clueless as to who could have done this.*

CHAPTER THIRTY-FIVE

Philadelphia, PA

As the police cars left the funeral home lot, Detective Mason interrupted Michael's thoughts. "Does Nicky drive?"

"Yes. I know she should drive to the precinct. I admit not being in one piece mentally at the present time."

"I would feel better if two of my officers follow you home when you leave our office later. This guy is still on the loose. We have no idea what his next move could be. I will call your precinct in Bucks County and see if they can get an officer or two to stay outside your home, at least for a few days. We need to share all the information we have and communicate back-and-forth. We need to work together and fast."

"Thanks. We appreciate all your help." Michael's voice was weak.

When they reached Detective Hall and Nicky, she got out of the police car and clung to him. "I am sorry, Babe."

On the drive to the hospital to see Jessica, he could not stop thinking about the two mutilated faces he had to witness of women he cared about. First, it was Britt and now Jessica. Then his thoughts returned to Becky and Ben. It will destroy them. As a father and business owner, he always felt in control. Yet, at that moment, he wasn't sure he could ever be that man again.

Nicky looked over at Michael. "I hope you know I'm here for you always." She reached for his hand after parking in the hospital lot. "This is ripping you apart. That's to be expected, but please don't feel it was your fault. I know that's how you think. You must let that go. A monster did this, and you have to concentrate on helping the police find him."

"I realize that. I'm okay."

Michael didn't want to leave Nicky in the car alone, so he suggested she go to the cafeteria in the hospital, while he popped in for a moment to see how Jessica was making out. She agreed.

At the front desk, he gave her name and asked for her room number.

"Are you a relative?"

"I'm her husband and she has been badly wounded today. Can I see her?"

"Have a seat over there. I will have a nurse come out to speak with you."

"Thank you."

"Mr. Pearson, I am Charlotte, your wife's nurse. She has only been here a short time so I can't tell you too much. Did you see her before she arrived?"

"Yes, I did, briefly. She's all banged up and I'm concerned."

"We are working with Mrs. Pearson to keep her as comfortable as possible. There are numerous tests that must be done right away. We do not like turning family away, but we need time to prepare her to have a family member visit in the CCU." The nurse checked her watch. "Tomorrow will be a much better time to visit. I would call first though."

"I understand. I want her to have the care she needs now, so I will do just that and call in the morning." Michael walked to the lobby where Nicky was sitting in a chair holding a bag of food and coffee.

"What happened?"

"Nothing. I can't see her until tomorrow. She is having tests and is in the CCU."

"That's rough, Honey."

"Yeh. What have you got there?"

"I picked up some donuts and coffee. As I sat here, though, I figured neither one of us is probably hungry."

"We can take off to chat with the detectives, then maybe munch on the donuts on the way home. Let's decide that later."

She handed him a mug of coffee.

The police department was in the center of the city, not far from the hospital. They arrived quickly, signed in and took a seat. Detective Mason came out and took them into a comfortable office. He gave them each a bottle of water and put the recorder in the center of the table between them.

"We are going to keep this brief. Whatever we discuss here, I will be sending to Detective Basil Gentry up in Bucks County."

The door opened and Detective Hall joined them. "You both need some rest." She sat across from the couple. "We advise you to contact your children and get them home with you, so you are all together where there will be protection."

Michael agreed. "I did think of that earlier. Good advice."

Detective Mason had been going over some notes. He looked up. "What I would suggest you do is tomorrow when you have had some sleep, go over every single male figure in your life. Pull out all those you buried through your business and consider if any of the families had hard feelings toward you or the service. Look at all your contacts over the years—especially the past few decades. Think hard if you might have had a quarrel over something big, or maybe turned someone away from your business."

"This is personal." Detective Hall interjected. "It could be as simple as passing another car too closely on the road, and they have road rage. Have you ever banged into another vehicle and continued on without stopping?"

"I will look into all of what you are suggesting, but I need to reveal to you a possible tip. I cannot connect it right now with my fuzzy brain."

"Let's have it." Detective Mason leaned forward.

"I don't know if you noticed that Britt McKenzie had bright red fancy shoes on when she was on the ground the day of her death. One of the shoes had dropped off in the fall I suppose and was lying next to her foot."

"Sure. We all saw that. Go on."

"Today, there was a police officer following the stretcher Jessica was on. He was carrying a see-through bag with the same bright red shoes that Britt had been wearing. I find that strange. In all the years I was in Jessica's life, I never saw her dress like that."

"*Now* we are getting somewhere." Detective Mason wrote something on the small pad in front of him.

"What's the connection between the two women, and who is this guy who might have known they were both connected to you, Michael? Were Jessica and Britt good friends?"

"Not at all. They met at Dana and Nick's over the recent holidays, but that was it. They did not travel in the same circles, and my thinking is that they would not be shopping together or lending one another shoes."

"Could this guy be someone working in your business who was friendly with Jessica, but had a beef with you?"

"No way. I know all of our employees and we all like one another. She does have a lover—Roger. But they have been together for many decades. I don't think he would do this to her."

"What about Britt? You told us she had a boyfriend. Do you have any idea who he could be?" Detective Mason did not share that they had already met her boyfriend, Bennett.

"Not a clue. She never mentioned his name."

"We have racked your brain enough. Get out of here and get some sleep. You too, Nicky." The detective stood and shook their hands. "Tomorrow you can go over all we have discussed. The connection is what you want to concentrate on first. Two of our officers will escort you home."

Detective Hall led them to the front of the building. "Thanks for coming in and telling us about the shoes. It may solve this crime in the end. Give us a call tomorrow if you come up with any possible suspects. In the meantime, we will be all over the apartment next door to your funeral home, Michael. Stay in touch."

"Will do."

Nicky took the wheel, and they started their drive home to Bucks County. There was a police car in front and back of their vehicle as promised.

By the time they reached their home, there were two police officers parked in front of their house. As soon as she parked, an officer came over to them. "We'll be here all night and other officers will take over in the morning."

"Thanks."

"We would like to check the inside of the house before you enter."

Nicky gave the officer her keys as Michael waved to the Philadelphia Police pulling away. They waited in silence in the car. She put her head on Michael's shoulder.

The two officers returned about ten minutes later, having checked the many rooms in the house on all floors. "It's all clear." The officers returned to their posts on the grounds.

Once in the house with their luggage, Michael grabbed clothes from his bag and took a long shower while Nicky made them toast and tea. They sat in the kitchen with their own thoughts for a good twenty-minutes before either of them said anything.

"Come Michael. Let's take our tea upstairs so I can get you into bed." Nicky kissed his forehead and they headed up the stairs to the master bedroom. She drew in a breath and held it as she stopped dead in their doorway. They viewed the mess in the room. It had been ransacked. Every drawer had been dumped on the floor, and covers, pillows, and sheets ripped to shreds, and thrown all over the floor. She couldn't imagine how anyone could get into the room. That door was always locked when they were not home. They had a vault in the room. What was strange is that it had not been touched.

"Obviously, the officer's downstairs never reached this floor. Don't you think they would have mentioned something to us, Michael, or reported it?"

He took off down the hallway to check the other rooms before going outside just as the two officers who were supposed to be outside their door were coming up the driveway.

"Where were you both when someone ransacked our master bedroom?"

"Sorry, there was a call about an accident down the road. We were told to take care of it."

"By whom? You were not supposed to leave us alone here. I heard your Chief of Police state that earlier."

The Police Chief, Danny Holder, had arrived and heard Michael's question. "How did this happen?" He looked over at his officers.

One of them replied, "Chief, you called us to get to that accident down the road, so we left. We assumed you would be sending two more guys over here."

"What are you talking about? I never called any of you." The Chief's face turned red. "I did not make any calls since I left this property earlier."

Michael could see that they were all confused at that point, so nothing was resolved.

"Do you suppose it was the guy who tried to kill my ex-wife tonight?"

"Why didn't I get a call about that?" the Chief asked.

"It happened in my funeral home in Philadelphia. He was in our apartment there. The detectives, Mason & Hall took care of it. They contacted Detective Gentry earlier. I guess he didn't get a chance to tell you yet."

The chief warned them, "You and your family need to be in a safe location now. This guy most likely found a way to contact my men and get them out of your home. He might have been hiding in your house before you returned. My suggestion is for you to get to a hotel tonight. Where are your children?"

Nicky had a hand on her mouth. "They are both out overnight."

"You should contact them, pick them up or whatever else you have to do and keep them with you at all times. I'll have two cars following you to the hotel should this guy be hanging around here."

The couple went back into the house to grab their luggage, with one of the officers following them.

As they packed the trunk of his car again, Michael pleaded with the Danny, the Chief of Police, "Please keep us informed about the house and this obvious murderer."

"I'll be in touch first thing tomorrow morning. Right now, I am on my way back to the office to find out what Gentry has learned."

Michael got on the road to first pick up Michaela a few houses down, then headed toward a hotel that was familiar to them, while Nicky called Becky. The two police cars followed.

CHAPTER THIRTY-SIX

Bucks County, PA

After receiving Nicky's call, Becky Pearson flew back to Bucks County, Pennsylvania, overnight and waited for her family at the airport. Her vacation had been cut short.

"There's Becky." Nicky pointed out where his daughter was standing with her luggage. They pulled over and Michael put everything in the trunk after hugs were shared.

Michael's phone lit up. "Hi Nick."

"We wanted to make sure you all got home safely yesterday."

"Yes. But we did have one problem when we arrived. It appears our stalker was in our home before us and ransacked our master bedroom."

"Oh, no!" Dana squealed. She was on the line also. "Are you all okay?"

"Yes. We are on our way to the precinct here to discuss our next move."

Nick took the phone again. "You can't live in that house now."

"We are staying at a local hotel, and the police are covering our home."

"We won't hear of that, Michael. You know there is plenty of room here for all of you. Please get your things together after your meeting and bring everyone back here. I insist." Dana's voice was cracking.

"I'll have to call you back. We are on our way to the precinct and anxious to hear what the detective here is going to do to catch this criminal."

"We have to get there before we go back to the hotel," he told Becky as he drove. "It appears this monster is not done with us yet. I am sorry you had to cut your trip short, but the detectives want us to all stay together until they catch him."

"Did he try to push you off the road again?"

While Michael concentrated on driving, Nicky filled Becky in with all the details about the suspect being in the house. "This guy appears to be more anxious to hurt us now. Yet the Police Chief tells us that between the Philadelphia detectives and his officers, they will get him and put him away."

Michael pulled up in the Bucks County police department lot. "I would like to ask all of you, but

Becky, to stay in the car or walk around if you wish for a bit until I speak with my daughter. I know this is a bad time, but it's only fair that Becky knows what to expect."

"What's going on, Dad?" she asked.

The others took a walk around the precinct while Michael told Becky about her mother's attack at the funeral home. He left out some details but didn't want her to hear it inside the department instead of from him.

She was shaken, "Is mom going to be okay? I mean, she's not in a coma or anything, right?"

"No, Sweetheart. Your mom is healing now, she's alert and might be in the hospital another week or so. We are going to stop there when we get into Philadelphia later today. You can see her then. I'm sorry this was so quick, but we have to get inside now. Are you okay?" He hugged her to him.

"Yes, thank you for telling me." They held hands as they joined the others and went into the station.

Detective Basil Gentry greeted them. "I will be responsible for your case now. Your detectives in Philadelphia gave me all the information they have, including the discussion you all had with them. I am sorry this criminal wounded one of your family members. I understand from Detective Mason, this guy has upped his game he's been playing with you on the road. An attempt at killing you and now your ex-wife, tells me his anger is elevated and he is more dangerous than ever."

Before they left to go back to the hotel, the detective went over all he knew. Then he asked Michael a lot of questions. They were about the same that Detective's Mason and Hall had asked.

"The chief agrees to have two officers around the clock positioned at your Bucks County home."

"We have been invited to my sister's home in Cape May, New Jersey for a few weeks, but we all have jobs. We plan to only enter our house together." *He purposely failed to mention that he has a gun in the house and wouldn't hesitate to use it if needed. He also has a license to carry and locks the gun up in the glove compartment of his car.*

"Good you have a plan, but still keep an eye out for this guy when you enter your house. I think we will catch him very soon. We have a lot more leads now. Our men will be hidden around the building. Remember, the one thing you must do is to stay together."

Michael stood. "We will. Thanks for your time, detective." They shook hands. The others thanked him. They left for the hotel to pack up their belongings and head to Philadelphia where they stopped by their funeral home. Michael and Becky ran in, checked on a few things, and closed the building down, including their attached apartment. They had all new locks and an alarm set up to go to the Philadelphia Police Department in case someone tried to break into the building.

"Did you get your mom's clothes she requested?"

"Yep, right here." She handed her dad the large suitcase which he put in the trunk of the car along with Becky's suitcase. Next, they drove to the hospital to visit Jessica. As they drove off Michael commented, "I hope they catch this guy now. We cannot lose too much time with our clients who may need our services."

Before they reached the hospital, they stopped for lunch a block from where Jessica was healing. A good brunch and coffee helped Michael and Becky to prepare for their visit with her.

There was small talk while they ate, but mostly silence. It wasn't a day to celebrate anything. "We will be quick," Michael told Nicky. "Are you sure you'll be okay here?"

"We are going to order an ice cream cone while we wait. We will not leave the restaurant," she promised.

Michaela gave him a big hug. "We will miss you." She gave her dad that adorable grin he loved. He hugged her back before leaving.

Becky and Michael were shocked when they entered Jessica's hospital room. She still looked terrible.

"Can you ask the nurse for more pain medicine?" Michael heard anxiety in her voice.

"I'll get someone, Mom."

While they waited a moment, Michael did note that Jessica's face had gone down more toward normal. "I'm afraid they haven't caught the suspect yet."

"I will never go back to the funeral apartment again. Roger suggested Ben and I move in with him. You are welcome also, Becky."

"Thank you, mom, but I will be staying with dad for now."

A nurse entered the room behind Becky. She gave Jessica a shot in the arm. "Can I get you anything else Ms. Pearson?"

"No. Thank you."

Michael was more than okay with Jessica's decision to move out of their home in Philadelphia. "Moving out is fine with me. I would prefer you do not talk to Ben about any of this. Right now, his mind should only be on healing from drugs and alcohol. As far as Ben knows, we are still together in the apartment."

"When I am out of here and feeling better, I want to go and see my son. You can't stop me, Michael."

"You can visit him. But if you love him, you cannot mention that we are divorcing, moving in with Roger, or anything else that would upset him. He needs to be told in little bits once he is out of the rehab. I suggest you leave Roger home when you visit Ben. He may not be aware your lover exists. You can tell him all you want after our family has a plan to ease him into learning about the changes we have made to his lifestyle. That will require a lot of discussion ahead of time, so we don't push him right back where he started because of us."

"Fine, I'll keep quiet."

"I will get all of your things out of the apartment, Mom."

"That's fine, Dear."

Becky laid a suitcase out on a chair next to the bed with items Jessica had requested from home. She took some out for her mom to see she had all of them on her list. "One of the aides should be able to help you with dressing when you are ready."

"Yes." Jessica laid her head back on the pillow. "They are very caring here. I just hope I won't be here longer than another week."

"Be patient. You don't want to leave before you are healed," Becky warned her. "We'll stop in and check on you when we can. I love you." She leaned over and kissed her cheek.

Michael glanced at her. "We'll see you soon. I am sorry this happened to you. Rest now and let Becky know if you need something."

They were almost to the door when Michael turned and looked back at her. "When did you purchase those bright red high-heeled shoes you had on when you were attacked?"

"I have never bought or worn red shoes. Why would you ask me that?"

"Never mind. I must have been mistaken. Get some rest."

They left the hospital and drove back to the restaurant. Nicky and Michaela were waiting outside on a bench. They hopped into the car. Becky gave the front seat to Nicky. The four of them headed for their home where Michael hoped to enjoy some time with his family. *He couldn't get his mind off his son, though. It was now only a month to his release from the rehabilitation center. He wanted them all to visit again, but he was afraid to drive up there, knowing the criminal has not yet been caught. What if he followed them and found a way to torture his son? He couldn't take that chance, but what would he tell Ben as to why they can't visit a month before they bring him home?*

CHAPTER THIRTY-SEVEN

Cape May, NJ

Jackson Hunter stopped by the bed and breakfast to offer Meg a job at his bookstore. He remembered when she and her friends stopped in a week or so ago, one of them mentioned her love of children's books.

Meg opened the door, shocked to see Jackson.

"Hi. I stopped by to offer you a job at my bookstore if you are interested. I remember your friend telling me you write and illustrate children's books. That's the area in the bookstore that I need to fill."

"Come in and have coffee with me. We can discuss it. I have been looking for a more permanent job. Taking care of the Bed & Breakfast is just temporary while Kate and Austin are on vacation."

Over the hot beverage and homemade cookies Meg had just brought from the oven, he told her about the position. "I would need you to start some children's programs we can have right in the bookstore. You can set up that area any way you wish . . . whatever works best for you and the children's group. I have a lot of children's books they can read inside or take home with them to return later."

"It sounds wonderful. I love children and books. I am thrilled to accept your offer. I thank you." Meg hugged her hands together and gave him a huge smile.

Jackson released a sigh. "I figured this would be my toughest challenge with the store, and then you came along."

"You are actually saving me a lot of time and worry. Recently returning to Cape May, I would have to look for work once Kate and Austin return home. Plus, I can't imagine having a better job. It's perfect. I won't let you down."

"I don't expect you will, Meg. Now tell me about this place. How many people do you have here?"

"One older man, Jose. He is staying for the week. I don't see too much of him as he likes to visit the shops and eat his meals out. He returns around six or so at night. Would you like more coffee or a cold drink?"

"I'm fine. I wouldn't mind a tour of this place since your one tenant is out. Would you mind?"

"Of course not. Follow me."

Meg started at the top floor where there was a large room and private bath. It looked out over the bay. Then they went down to the second floor, where there was another large room with two beds, and a smaller room down the hall with one bed. These rooms had to share a hallway bath. Next, she showed him a small room with one bed and a small bath on the first floor. It was slightly above the bed and breakfast owner's private area below, which went from there to the back of the building. Kate and Austin had a separate apartment attached to the living room and kitchen areas, with a wide screened in porch.

"If I chose to rent here until I find a house, I would request the one at the top with the private bath and view of the bay," Jackson stated as they returned to the kitchen.

Meg filled their cups again. "That's the best choice. I don't want to pry, but I am curious. Are you thinking of staying here for a while?"

"Possibly. I live with my sister at the moment. We are from North Dakota. She is a few decades older than me and couldn't take the cold weather there anymore. She moved here a few years ago. After I retired from working in real estate, I traveled through a few countries and, as a book lover, I decided to move here and open a bookstore."

"Have you looked at any houses yet?"

"A few. Then I got involved with the store. My sister has a fiancé living with her. Her house is small, and I feel like I'm in the way. That's what gave me the idea to stay here until I find something I like."

"I am sure Kate and Austin would love to have you."

A quick thought ran through her mind of how Jackson's looks were easy on the eyes. She loved his steady disposition—at least the two times she was in his company.

"I had better get going. I've taken up enough of your time on a Saturday. Here's my number." Jackson wrote on a small tablet he had in his pocket and handed the paper to her. "Let me know when you can start at the bookstore. But feel free to take some time off once your friends return home. I can wait."

Her excitement showed in her constant smile and her hands rubbing together as if she had just won a lottery. "Wait." She gave him one of her business cards with her phone number on it. "Let me know if you decide to move in here. I will have the room on the top ready for you. Have a good evening."

"Thank you." He took the card from her and closed the front door behind him.

Her fears of not finding a job were over. She knew she was lucky to have connected with a great boss, and she couldn't wait to start. But she had two more weeks to care for the Bed & Breakfast, so she began tidying up the place again.

Meg had just gotten out of the shower when she received a call from Kate.

"Hello, I'm surprised you took time to speak with me when you have that lovely view," Meg teased.

"It is beautiful here. As much as I would love to chat with you, I am calling to ask a favor. Could you possibly stay at the B & B an extra week? It is so amazing here, and we ran into old friends who are vacationing as well. We'd like to spend time with them before we leave."

"No problem. Go and enjoy. Everything here is fine."

"Thanks so much, Meg. We'll make it up to you. Love you." Kate ended the call.

She agreed to stay, sure that Jackson wouldn't mind since he didn't insist on a specific date to start her job. Plus, it could mean more time spent learning about the bookstore and her new boss.

CHAPTER THIRTY-EIGHT

Cape May, NJ

The next morning, Meg was working on one of her children's books after breakfast. Her phone buzzed before she began to write.

"Hello."

"Hi. It's Jackson. I hope I'm not calling you too early, but I wanted to be sure you didn't rent out that top room yet."

"I have not. What's happening?"

"Whenever it's ready, I will take it. Let me know when to pack up my things."

"That's wonderful. You can take it over whenever you wish. Were you thinking of after work tonight? Or maybe tomorrow morning before you head to work?"

"Great idea. How about seven tonight? I will bring dinner, so don't knock yourself out."

"Sounds good to me."

After she got off the phone and poured herself a cold drink, she called Dana to share her news. "How is everyone?"

"We are fine. How about you? Sounds like you are full of cheer this morning."

"You will never guess who will be moving into the Bed & Breakfast temporarily until he finds a house here."

"Let's see . . . do I know him?"

"You met one time recently."

"Hmmm. Oh . . . Jackson Hunter?"

"You are correct!"

"Doesn't he have a home in Cape May?"

She repeated what Jackson had told her about living with his sister and how crowded it had become.

"I see. You can't blame him for not wanting to interfere with their time. I think Kate and Austin will like having him there until he finds the right house."

"You didn't hear the best part. He offered me a job at his bookstore. I will be working with children there and planning programs for them. Of course, we will also be reading books and encouraging them to take some home with them."

She had to pull the phone away from her ear while Dana left out a loud squeal. "You lucked out with this guy, Meg."

"I owe it all to you since you were the one who told him I write the books, remember?"

"That's right, I did. Tell me more about him."

"He seems to be calm, considerate, interesting, and I can bet most women call him eye-candy."

Dana laughed. "Sounds like you might have found the whole package."

"Let's not go that far. Yet, I am sure I will enjoy having him around here and working with him at the store."

"I am happy for you, my friend. You need this in your life right now. Hey, why don't you bring Jackson to dinner tonight? We can get to know him better. After all, we all read books and his bookstore is closer than going to the mall. You know Nick will be at his store a lot. Let's get together and make him feel at home."

"Are you sure?"

"Yes. Let him know we would love to have him and we're preparing a place for both of you at the table, so he can't refuse."

"Okay, I'll let you know in a few hours."

"By the way, everything is fine with Laney, Charlie and the baby. He is adorable," Dana told her. "Charlie wants you to know he is going to send you photos of Glen whenever he can, without Laney knowing it. He feels bad to go behind her back, but Charlie is sensitive, as you know. He can't bear the suffering you are going through while your daughter refuses to see or acknowledge you at this time."

Meg couldn't speak for a moment, overwhelmed with pleasure.

"Are you okay?"

Tears slid down her cheeks. "I'm sorry, Dana, I lost it for a moment. Your son is the sweetest man I know. You did a great job raising him. Please let him know I could never thank him enough for doing this. I tried to call Laney last week, but it went to voicemail and she never returned my calls."

"Allow more time to pass, and she will realize just how much she needs and loves you. Hold onto that and the photos you get of your grandson. You know I will keep you in the loop."

"You are wonderful. I love you and your family. Talk to you later."

After making a fresh pot of coffee for herself and putting some classical music on, Meg returned to illustrating her latest children's book to keep her mind busy. Otherwise, she would spend an hour crying over something she could do nothing about . . . her daughter disowning her as a mother. With the current book she was working on, she decided to name the main character 'Glen' just like her new grandson she hoped to meet one day. She dried her eyes and hit Jackson's number to tell him about their dinner invitation for later that evening.

"Did you forget we planned on my moving into the Bed & Breakfast tonight? I already ordered our dinner."

"It must have slipped my mind. No problem. I will call Dana and get a rain check."

"Okay, see you at seven."

Meg called her. "I apologize, but we cannot make it to dinner. It appears I forgot that Jackson is moving into the Bed & Breakfast tonight and already ordered our dinner to bring with him."

"You enjoy your time with Jackson. I would have made that choice also. Next time, we will set up dinner ahead instead of giving you such short notice. Enjoy!"

She was glad her friend accepted her apology.

Jackson arrived at the bed and breakfast at exactly seven p.m., as planned. Meg had tidied up the top room and bath for him. She made a pot of coffee and put fruit in a bowl on the table.

"Welcome to your new home."

"Thank you. It's only temporary until I find a house here."

Jackson handed her their dinner, which was eggs benedict and steak. "I hope you like my choices."

Meg pulled off the lid and gasped. *She had no idea he had such good taste.* "This is one of my favorites, but I rarely get it. Thanks."

"I should be thanking you for all you are doing for me."

While she set up the rest of the table, he took his things up to his room. When he returned to the kitchen, they chatted all through the meal and during coffee.

"You are getting quite a following, Jackson. I love seeing so many people are interested in your place."

"Things are looking up, aren't they? It will help to have you there to bring in the people. You will have great communication skills, Meg. People just seem to cling to you."

"Now you are going to make me blush. Why don't we take our dessert and coffee out to the screened-in porch? I love sitting out there in the evenings. It's peaceful and relaxing."

"Sure. I'll carry the dessert." She followed him out with the coffee on a tray. They spent two hours chatting about the bookstore, the benefits of living in Cape May and more. They suddenly realized it was ten p.m.

Jackson helped Meg clean up the table. Then he turned toward the stairway to his room. "I better get upstairs and test out my new sleeping quarters."

"Go up and get comfortable. I'll clean up the kitchen. See you in the morning."

CHAPTER THIRTY-NINE

Cape May, NJ

After a great afternoon in Philadelphia with Michael's family meeting Laney, Charlie and the baby, he handed out their gifts. Then they headed to the Campanella's home for a visit.

Nicky was in love with their son. "He is so adorable. I love his bright red hair."

"I think Glen looks a lot like his dad, but you are right about the red hair. He can thank his mom for that. Do you think his eyes will be green soon?" Becky wondered aloud. She looked over at her new sister sitting next to her in the back seat. "What do you think, Michaela?"

"He's cute. I was hoping to play with him longer." She giggled.

"Don't worry, Honey. We will see them again. We are all family now," Michael assured her. He looked in his rear-view mirror to see her big grin. As she moved her head aside, he noted a black car behind them. He tried to join in on the conversation but was distracted by the possibility it was his stalker again. He decided to suddenly pull over to the right, forcing the black car to pass them. But instead, the driver pulled over in back of Michael's vehicle and waited. They both stayed in that spot for about three minutes, when the others noticed they were not moving. *He wanted so badly to get out of his car and rush back there to bang on his darkened windows.*

"What's going on, Dad?" Becky asked. "Why are we sitting here?"

"It's nothing. I was going to make a quick phone call but changed my mind." He pulled the car back onto the road, noting that the driver did the same and was still following him. He didn't want to alarm the women, so he kept going with a close eye on the tail. His hands were moist now, beads of sweat forming on his forehead, and he was breathing faster than usual.

"Honey, are you okay?" Nicky sat beside him.

"Sure. I feel warm though." He lowered his window, and she did the same.

Right before they reached the Campanella's home, the black car took off in another direction.

His fiancé reached for his free hand. "That was a lovely afternoon, but I am glad we are back in Cape

May. If I didn't love our home so much, I would try and interest you all into moving here. It's beautiful."

"Maybe someday when we are older," Michael teased. "I believe it's called retirement."

They were in the lovely Victorian house again. The women went off to share their afternoon with Dana.

Michael took Nick aside to let him know he and his family would be returning to Bucks County that night. "I didn't want to upset the women, especially Dana after all she went through with my brother. I believe the guy who has been tailing me did so almost our whole trip here from Philadelphia. I don't want any trouble for you guys. You've been through enough. You don't want this jerk in your life."

Nick scratched his head. "If the guy tailed you here, he most likely will follow you back to your home. He probably just pulled away a short distance to wait for you to leave again. We are secure here. I'll contact the police. Plus, we have an alarm that goes right to the station and this place is locked up tight at night. Then you can at least go home in the daylight tomorrow if you wish."

"I don't know." *Michael wanted to leave. But he caved in when Nick made his speech to convince him to stay. He's probably right that the guy could be outside the community waiting for them in the darkness.*

"Get some coffee and alert your detectives in Philadelphia and Bucks County that he is tailing you again."

Michael finally gave in, thanked him and explained to the women he was too tired to drive back home at night. They all retired for the evening.

As usual, Dana could not sleep. She went back downstairs to make a warm glass of milk, then returned up to their art studio on the second floor. She sat on the deck overlooking the ocean. It was past dusk, yet thanks to the bright moon, she could still make out a man's figure on the beach. He was facing the ocean. Grabbing their binoculars left out on the table beside her, she was shocked to see the man now facing in her direction. *This can't be happening to us again. Matthew is now deceased. It's not possible!*

******

The next morning during breakfast Michael received a call back from the detectives in Bucks County that it was not safe to return home. With his permission last night, Detective Gentry got some men out there to put in a special alarm that would go from every window, door and surrounding ground to the police station should anyone try to enter. "We want to catch this guy while he is tailing you again, Michael. Do you think you could spend two more days there in Cape May while we try to catch him breaking into your home? If he is hiding out there, he may try to beat you up here and be waiting inside for you all to arrive. We have a plan and want to move quickly."

"Okay. But just two days, right? We all have to get back to work."

"We will set it up now and keep you aware of what is happening."

When Michael got off the phone, Nick asked, "Are you sure you will be comfortable going home?"

"That was Detective Gentry from our precinct in Bucks County. It appears they have a plan in place to try and catch this lowlife. I agreed to stay away from the house for two more days. He swore he would let me know how it's going and when we can return. Are you sure you don't mind?"

"Of course not," Dana chimed in. "We want you to stay until this is resolved. If they think they can catch this guy now, the nightmare will finally be over for all of you."

"We can't hide forever. I appreciate all you have done for us. We are lucky to be in such a caring family."

Michaela spoke up, "But what about school?"

"Honey, it will only be two more days, and your grades are excellent. I don't think you have anything to worry about."

Becky agreed with her. "I hope they catch the criminal this time. We have to get back to Philadelphia to attend to our clients."

"You are right, Becky. I admit feeling restless to get back to the funeral home too. Yet, I feel that if our precinct is willing to set up a plan that finally catches this guy, we will all get our lives back."

Louisa came down with Emily Rose and handed the baby to her uncle. "This is Uncle Mike," she told Emily.

Michael kissed her forehead. "She has really grown. You are a cutie-pie." He tickled her belly and she giggled. Then he turned toward his daughters. "These are your cousins, Michaela and Becky."

The toddler reached for Michaela's long braids and pulled one. She gently lifted it from Emily's little hand and placed it on top of her head. Everyone laughed.

Michael handed the baby to Nicky. Emily Rose touched her face. After telling her how adorable she was and kissing her cheek, she returned Emily Rose to her grandmother. She placed her in her swing in their family room.

"I am sorry you have to leave so soon."

"We are not leaving, Mom. While you were upstairs the detective from Bucks County called that we should stay a bit longer. They have a plan to try and catch the psycho tailing us again."

She hugged her son. "That's wonderful. We should all pray that it works this time. Let's celebrate with this yummy cake I made this morning."

CHAPTER FORTY

Bucks County, PA

That afternoon, while Michael and his family were enjoying their time with the Campanella's, the detectives in Michael and Nicky's home were setting up a plan in their house. Officers were hidden around the property in among the shrubbery. They wore clothes that blended in with nature.

"The only thing the killer should be able to notice will be the loving couple, resembling Michael and Nicky, in their home acting out a love scene with a lot of squealing." Detective Gentry told his team. "Once we note this guy sees them inside, thanks to the front of their home in glass, it should draw him to the front door. When the couple hears us say "Go!" they will run upstairs to the master bedroom and lock the door while he is trying to get in the front. The rest is up to us. Eyes and ears open and make sure you have your weapons ready. Do not leave your posts at any time until we get this guy. We are fortunate that Michael decided to purchase a new car recently but kept his old one out front of his house. I have no doubt, with Michael's car outside here, the bright lights inside, and a couple this guy can see through the front windows making love, we will nail him. It's a perfect setting."

Danny, Chief of Police got hold of Gentry. "How's it going there? Is everyone okay? It's been a few hours now. Soon it will be dusk. How are you going to see this guy?"

Detective Gentry could imagine the Chief's face and neck soaked with sweat by now. He was overweight and easily worried about everything.

"As you know, we had to check every room on all floors and closets in this house to make sure this loser wasn't already hiding inside. He knows the Pearson's are in Cape May right now since he followed them there earlier. He may be on his way here right now to await their arrival home." He took a swig of water.

"Listen up people. We need to keep our earplugs in at all times, including the actor and actress, so we all know what is happening. Do not talk once he's here. Let's put this guy away for good! As soon as we have him chief, I'll contact you before we bring him in to the office."

Outside, Gentry laid low, but not too low that he wouldn't be able to see the criminal arrive. The lights that were dim suddenly became brighter through the front window. The couple was in place.

An hour later, a male figure appeared. "He's here," Gentry whispered to them. "There's no car. He is stooped down in the front of the window watching the couple." *Gentry knew he had to use the exact moment the criminal was distracted with the front door lock, so the pretend lovers could get upstairs before he realized they were gone.* A few seconds passed. Then the guy crept over to unlock the front door. Gentry whispered to the couple "Go".

The lights in the front room went out. The detective stuck his gun in the criminal's back and turned on his flashlight. "Don't make a move or you're dead." Another officer joined them and put the male in handcuffs. *Gentry thought the suspect looked taller than what he had been told.*

When the officer turned the suspect around after handcuffing him, he faced the detective.

"Please don't shoot me! I'm only here because Becky told me to use these keys when I arrived from the airport. My name is Dane Watson."

"What?" The officer searched him and found a small wallet he handed over to Gentry. When he opened it up, there was his name, passport papers, Becky

Pearson's photo with this guy, a blonde and a few credit cards. "Take the cuffs off."

"Why?" The officer was confused.

"He's not our killer."

"Killer?" The young man turned white, even with his bronze tan. "Becky's okay, right?"

"Yes. The entire family is okay at another location. I suggest you call Ms. Pearson and get the story. This is a stake-out you walked into, so you cannot stay here right now. I'm surprised Becky would send you here knowing what is happening."

Becky's friend kept nervously touching his hair and pulling on his ear. "She must have forgotten she had given me the keys when we were on vacation together a few months ago. We haven't talked in a while. I got tied up in some business dealings in Europe and barely had time to speak with her while I was there. It was dark when I got here, so I thought I'd use the key and surprise her."

"Well, you are free to go, Mr. Watson. You do have a car?"

"Yes. I left it down the road because I didn't want to pull up this late at night and scare her."

"Too late for that. Okay, be on your way."

"Thanks. Sorry for the intrusion."

The police team stayed overnight and into the next evening of darkness, but the killer never showed up.

The detective contacted Michael Pearson to let him know. "I'm sure you understand that we have to get back to policing other problems also. You will have to decide if you want to return here and stay or find another place to live in case this guy is resting for a while to throw us off. If we get a call, we will respond. Although, I would be surprised if he gave up. Should you decide to return here, make sure you keep up that expensive security system you now have throughout your home. You should also register for a weapon, as long as you know how to use it."

"I have one, and I do know how to use it, detective. I can't imagine moving us unless it is to Philadelphia where our business is probably failing at this point. We are not there as much as we should be because of this mess."

"That might be a good idea. You don't have to sell your home here, just not live in it for now. You have good security in your business as well. We'll stay in touch with Detectives Mason and Hall and work together."

"I will discuss it with my family and see what they want to do." Michael let out a heavy sigh. "Thank you and thank the chief."

"I'll do that. Let us know later what you decide."

He didn't want to tell the others until the next day. He had to get his own thoughts together first.

******

Detective Mason accepted a call from Detective Gentry from Bucks County about his team's efforts to catch Michael's stalker at his home and failed.

"I am sorry to hear that. Carla and I were just going over a plan ourselves. You weren't around last year when Dana and her family went through a lot of heartache and terror. Michael was involved also. I won't get into that now. We are hoping to meet with the Campanella's sometime tomorrow. We would like them to invite their friends and family who were familiar with all that transpired last year," Detective Mason explained.

"That sounds good. How many were part of that turmoil?"

"Pretty much everyone in their family, plus some outside. We think with all of them together, we might be able to figure out who this guy is and where he lives."

"You know Michael is there now. I believe he is staying overnight," Detective Gentry offered.

"Great, maybe we can make it for tomorrow afternoon then. Feel free to join us if you wish."

"I'll have to see what my schedule is like tomorrow, but either way, please let me know if you make any headway with this criminal."

"A text is on its way with Dana's address in Cape May, should you be able to get there around noon."

"Okay, I'll do my best." Gentry broke the connection.

Detective Hall hit Dana's home number. "Hello, Dana. How are you?"

"We are well, sitting here with my brother, Michael, who I don't see enough. He is talking about his safety and guessing when this nightmare is going to end with an arrest."

"Excellent. This is why we are calling you today. As bad as this suggestion will be to all of you probably trying to forget last year, we are asking you to discuss with us anyone you remember being in your life at that time who could be holding a grudge."

"Detective Mason here, Dana. I just spoke to Detective Gentry. I suppose Michael told you by now that their efforts failed in their attempt to catch this guy at Michael's Bucks County home. We would like to try something as well. I am sorry it could bring up memories you all may not want to remember. But having this over, and the criminal locked up, might be worth the sorrowful recall."

"Sure. What do you have in mind?" Nick was online too.

"Get your friends and family together. We need anyone who was around last year and might have met or witnessed others you all came in contact with at some point. We will come to you, rather than all of you make that long trip. Do you think your friends and family would be up for this and available tomorrow around noon?"

"We will make sure they are," Nick assured him. "It will be Sunday, so not a workday. Most of them live here in Cape May."

Dana cut in, "I'll call them today and make sure they are available. Then we'll get back to you. I'd rather you not make a trip if we can't get them together. But like my husband indicated, it would be unusual for them to say no to something this important."

"Wonderful. Thank you both. Try and keep Michael there if possible. He might be a big help since he was the one who connected the red shoes on all the criminal's victims."

"I'm sure he will want to be a part of this."

"Thanks. Let us know." Detective Mason ended the call.

CHAPTER FORTY-ONE

Cape May, NJ

Exactly at noontime, Detectives Mason and Hall pulled up in front of Nick and Dana's Victorian home.

"Now, this is living." Carla had her head out the window and stared straight up toward the veranda.

They vacated the car and Brock looked up. "Wow, I wouldn't want to have to climb these steps every day."

"I would climb double that to live at the shore." Carla's eyes widened at the sight of the ocean across from the Campanella home. She turned and put her arm in Brocks. "Let's go old man." She led the way up the long rising set of stairs to their front door.

Meantime, Brock was tall enough to be a professional ball player, and strong enough to climb the stairs himself, but he liked Carla's attention.

"You do realize I am only eight years older than you, right?"

"Hello," Dana yelled down to them. "Sorry about the climb. I forgot to tell you it's easier coming in the back way where there are less stairs."

"That's okay." Detective Mason took a deep breath as they reached the top of the stairs. "My partner here will tell you I can use the exercise."

"Come in and rest. We have hot coffee."

"Good to hear." The detectives were led into the dining room. Detective Mason noticed Nicky and Michaela at the table. "I don't believe we've met these lovely ladies yet."

Michael spoke up. "This is Nicky Collins, my fiancé, and our daughter, Michaela Pearson." He put his arm around their daughter and smiled at her.

"Nice to meet you both."

Dana walked over to Michaela. "You can play with Emily Rose if you wish, instead of listening to our boring conversations."

"Okay, great." She went into the adjoining room with Dana. "Hi Emily Rose. I came to play with you."

Detective Hall addressed Michael while Dana was away from the table. "Your timing is perfect. We are pleased you could be a part of this get-together. How are you feeling?"

When Dana returned to the table, Kate applauded her for giving Michaela time to play with Emily Rose.

Yet, she knew it was because Dana felt their conversations were not appropriate for her to sit in on.

Then Michael replied to Detective Hall, "I'm fine. It's a real challenge to be on the road. I never know when this monster will show up again."

Detective Hall agreed. "Let's hope we can put our heads together and think back to last year. We should have only male suspects in our thoughts. I would guess it would not be a woman driving a large vehicle in the manner in which you described to us recently."

Dana agreed. "Michael describes the vehicle as being huge. He feels the driver surely has no fears of even harming himself which is reckless."

Louisa poured their coffee, with plates for their danish and lovely little sandwiches with different lunchmeat and cheese in them. Then she took her seat at the table. "How can we help you detectives?"

The recorder for the middle of the dining room table was placed by Detective Hall. "Here's an example: We need to hear from each one of you about any contact you had with Jean Walters. We mention her name only because the majority here met and knew her in some way."

Noticing the "oh—no!" looks around the table, other than for Dana, Detective Mason suggested she start. "Why don't you speak first since you knew Jean Walters really well?"

Dana slowly began to talk. "I did know Jean Walters rather well. We met when she saved my life last year. We became good friends after that. In fact, I invited her to our wedding in Bar Harbor, Maine. She also accepted my invitation to join us with our trip to New York. She was a lovely woman. I will never forget her. As for her son, Brian Walters, I never met him. But when his mother was murdered, he called to let me know that. I would probably recognize his voice if I heard it again, but I have never met him."

"Same here," Nick offered. "When Dana got the news from Jean's son, she dropped the phone and went into a state of shock. As the paramedics were getting her ready to be taken to the hospital, I quickly re-dialed the number of the recent caller to see who put her in that state and why. Brian Walters told me who he was and that he called to let Dana know his mother was gone. He broke up a lot during that short call, but I might be able to remember his voice."

Kate spoke next, "I met Jean Walters through Dana. We spent an entire day together . . . the three of us, at Dana's Chalet in the mountains. That is when she invited Jean to her wedding. I remember Jean talked a lot about her son and his family. She told us she had a young granddaughter. When her mother had to go somewhere, Jean would spend time with the child named Penny." She put her hand to her forehead, trying to remember more about

Jean. "Oh, I was also in her home. She offered me to come in for coffee when I was dropping her off. I spent about an hour there. She showed me photos of her family. I did get to see her son's photo close up on her refrigerator. I might be able to pick him out of a line-up, if needed. Although I never heard his voice or met him."

"Do any of you know where he lives in Philadelphia?"

They looked over at one another. No one knew his location.

Detective Hall pushed a number on her phone. "Marcy, can you make some calls on a Brian Walters, most likely living in Philadelphia, male, about five-five, stocky, and thick dark hair. Check also for a criminal record. Try and get his address. He has a wife and young daughter. Let us know as soon as you find anything on them. Thanks."

Detective Mason explained, "I am sure you all wonder why Brian Walters became a suspect. We were lucky to get his description from a gentleman recently who knew Ms. McKenzie. He was in his car outside her condominium ready to leave from a visit with her, when he noticed a male rushing across the street and right in through her unlocked front door. He noted that Britt was dressed up when he was up there, and felt she was waiting for this guy. Since he had an appointment he couldn't afford to miss, he drove away. He gave us the time on his watch that day which showed three minutes before Ms. McKenzie's death, according to the coroner's report. We didn't want to give his name to you so we could see if any of you already suspected Walters as a criminal."

Dana added, "I can't believe we never thought of him before this. Revenge seems to be what he was looking for all this time. I should have put it together."

"It's not so easy to do that since there are so many others like him out there in our society. Don't blame yourself, Dana. I wish we had thought of him earlier. Detective Hall came up with his name the other day when we were discussing the red shoes he left at each place where he harmed his victims. Putting it all together, it made sense that he might not have known Britt McKenzie, but he knew that Michael had some kind of relationship with her." He looked over at Michael. "The same for Jessica. He knew you lived there with her at the funeral home apartment and assumed she was important to you. Then he came after you and your family . . . hoping to get them out of your life."

"It appears that he doesn't just want to kill you, but everyone who you love. It's his way of getting revenge for you killing his mother."

Michael finally spoke up. "You are right, Detective Hall. It is amazing that none of us thought of him before this. He probably saw the news a while ago, stating that I was released from prison because my family proved I was not the one who killed Brian Walter's mother. We all found out later that the real murderer used my name to do his crimes."

Detective Hall's phone buzzed. "Hello, can I help you?"

"It's Marcy. I spoke with Brian Walter's wife, Jennifer. She claims that her husband left the family about seven months ago. All he could concentrate on was his mother's death. He had a newspaper showing the killer being released from prison. That set him off."

"Text me the address right away, Marcy. We need to pay her a visit."

"Time to go," Detective Mason got up from his chair. "Thank you all for your help. This is our guy. We will get him this time and be in touch."

Detective Hall thanked them also. She gave them all an artist sketch of a description their precinct was given of what the possible killer looked like. The detectives left right away, heading for Jennifer Walters home in Philadelphia.

"Wow, that was mind-boggling!" Austin was all fired up since he had never heard about all that went before his time with Dana's family.

"All this time, and who would have thought of the Walters family having a criminal." Nick had his hands behind his neck to stretch.

After they all agreed Michael and his family must stay a few more days to give the detectives time to catch the real suspect, their doorbell rang.

Louisa opened the door. "Meg, come in. I am so happy to see you." They hugged.

"This is Jackson Hunter, Louisa."

"It's nice to meet you, Mr. Hunter. I hear you have a great bookstore."

Nick left the table and went right to the living room. "Did I hear the word bookstore? Nice to meet you. I will be your most profitable customer."

Dana walked over behind him. "He is an avid reader of every subject you can imagine Jackson. You will probably be a millionaire by the time my husband buys all your books."

"I am selective of some," he told his wife. She laughed out loud.

Michael came down the stairs from checking on Emily Rose.

Meg hugged him. "Are you surprised?"

"I am happy to see you here."

"This is my friend, and boss, Jackson Hunter. He owns the new bookstore."

"Nice to meet you. When are you guys leaving for your trip?"

"Very soon, which is why I wanted to get here to say goodbye to all of you. I should think we won't be there too long since I hear the snow is brutal once it hits that area. Jackson has some business there and asked me to come along." She smiled up at him.

"Come in and have a seat at the table. I assume you are a coffee drinker, Jackson?" Louisa was holding two cups of coffee.

"I am. Thank you. What's new with all of you?"

Nick scratched his head. "Get comfortable. That's a loaded question."

CHAPTER FORTY-TWO

Cape May, NJ

The Bed and Breakfast had no new vacationers since Jose left, other than for Jackson's room. Meg felt it was a good opportunity for her to spend some time at the bookstore if she could get Louisa to take her place. Meg knew she had taken over the Bed & Breakfast before when the couple was away.

"Of course, I'll do it," Louisa assured Meg. "We just finished breakfast. Let me change and I'll be right over."

"No rush. I am grateful you are willing to help me out."

"I am happy that you have the opportunity to land a job where you can feed your passion. See you in a half hour."

Louisa arrived in less than that. Meg opened the front door to greet her.

"Hi. That was quick. You don't speed in Cape May, do you?" she teased.

"Never. My motorcycle wouldn't hold up too well if I did."

They had a good laugh. "You've been here before, haven't you?"

"Many times. It's a beautiful place. I am happy you asked me to do this. With Dana home a lot now, she cares for Emily Rose more than I do, except for our rocking session at night before the baby's bedtime. Don't rush yourself. I can do this any days you would need me."

"You are sweet, Louisa. Dana is lucky to have a mom like you." Meg hugged her. "I made a fresh pot of coffee and left out the goodies. Feel free to eat or drink anything you wish. Call me if you have any problems." She handed her the phone number. "It's been pretty quiet since Kate and Austin left. Jackson is not here during the day either. You have the place to yourself unless we get a new vacationer."

"Enjoy the bookstore and that handsome guy you have for a boss." Louisa rolled her eyes, as a smile spread across her face.

"Ha-ha. I don't think either of us are ready for what you are thinking, my friend. I'll be back about five if that's okay."

"I'll be here. Don't worry about the time."

Meg walked from the Bed & Breakfast to the bookstore, which was about four blocks. It was a sunny day. When she arrived, she went right into the store.

Jackson greeted her. "Hey, great to see you, Meg. Who is running the Bed and Breakfast?"

"Dana's mom, Louisa. She is such a nice lady. We are not busy, so I thought I would join you today and learn some things about your store."

"Wonderful! First, I know you would love coffee."

"You already know me too well." She blushed. Once they finished their coffee and chatted a bit about Meg's responsibilities there, Jackson stood. "Let me give you the grand tour."

"I'm ready." She had even brought a tablet and pen to take notes. "Lead the way, Boss."

"This is the children's area. As you will note, everything is in a circle. I like that because it draws the children in to socialize about the books they like. What do you think?"

"It's a great idea. I'm all for this type of layout. It's also spacious compared to what I imagined it to be in this section. I think from the front of the bookstore, the building appears smaller, when really it is not."

"You are observant. I think you will be teaching me instead of the other way around." He chuckled. "The children's bathroom is right here across from the reading room. As you can see, all the children's books are in a circle as well with eight shelves leading almost to the ceiling. Yes, we do have a way to get those top ones down."

"That was my next question."

"Over there in the corner is a pole long enough to reach up and grab any book you might need. Now, let's sit on one of these chairs and you tell me about any plans or thoughts on programs you would like to implement for the children."

"I actually have a number of ideas. First, until the children get used to me and feel comfortable here, I thought that maybe twice a week . . . Monday and Wednesday . . . we could have a program for the different age groups two hours a day. Then they get to take two books home. At the end of the week, we will have a full program where all of the children come together to talk about their favorite book and why."

"That's a good plan, Meg. I like it. When can you start?"

"Well, Louisa offered to spend time at the Bed & Breakfast whenever I need her. As long as no one new has come in to stay with us before Kate and Austin return home, she might agree to my return again tomorrow. There's a lot of decision-making and planning on paper exactly how this is going to begin, don't you think?"

"Definitely. Let me know. If you can make that happen, it will be great. If not, I understand and

maybe we can discuss it more when I am at the Bed
& Breakfast. Now, make yourself at home. Walk around
and check out the books. If you want to change anything . . . even the children's layout with the chairs,
feel free. This is your room now. You're the boss
here. If you have any questions at all, just holler. I'll
be in and out of these other two adult rooms or in the
office. In fact, let me take you through those areas
before you get started."

******

By the time Meg returned to the Bed and Breakfast
and thanked Louisa for taking over while she learned
more about the bookstore, she was exhausted.

"I'll be on my way. I can see you worked hard today."

"Sorry, but you are right, Louisa. I am tired. It's
a lot to take in at one time, you know?"

"I do. Get some rest, Honey."

Meg opted for a hot shower as soon as Louisa left.
She dressed and planned to take a nap when the front
door opened. Kate and Austin stood in front of her
with their luggage.

"This is an unexpected surprise," she hugged them
both. "What happened?"

Kate walked into the kitchen with Meg following.
"Austin got a call from his boss that he was desper-
ately needed back to work this week. It seems that
two of the builders took ill with a virus, so they need

my husband back." Kate rolled her eyes and began brewing a new pot of coffee.

Austin came into the room. "Thanks for taking care of the place, Meg. We appreciate the great vacation we had, but I have to get back to work tomorrow."

"It was fun. Although you only had two clients. One of them, Jackson Hunter, is still here on the top floor. It's temporary until he finds a house he likes in this area. I hope that's okay."

Austin loved the idea. "It's great to have another male around here." He kissed his wife's forehead, picked up the suitcases, and took off to their spacious suite in the back of the bed and breakfast.

The friends sat at the table and shared their adventures of the last three weeks before Meg excused herself, begging exhaustion and left for home.

CHAPTER FORTY-THREE

Cape May, NJ

After Meg had been working in the bookstore for a few weeks, Jackson gave her more responsibility with some office work, and had taken her out to dinner to celebrate. She knew he really appreciated how much time and energy she put into every day with the children.

This particular morning brought in a customer she never realized until later would change both their lives. She was putting on a pot of coffee when she heard their entrance bell at the front door. She walked to the front of the shop just in time to greet an older gentleman standing inside.

"Welcome, Sir." She shook his hand. "I'm Meg Carson. How can we help you today?"

"Paul Jenkins." He grinned at her. "Call me Paul. I'm looking for some good books to read while my wife and I are vacationing here this month. Any suggestions?"

"Follow me. What are you interested in reading, Paul?"

"We like crime mysteries. I'm pretty good at figuring out the 'who done it' person. My wife reads the same book after me, then we write on paper who we believe did the crime. She only beat me on two books out of over a hundred so far this year."

"That's amazing. Have you worked in or studied criminal justice in the past?"

"No, but we don't miss any of them on television."

"Let me take you back to the adult books. We have a vast section of mystery, criminal, and psychological thrillers."

"Wow, this is great," the gentleman picked up one of the crime books.

As she poured herself a cup of coffee at the front of the shop, Jackson came walking into the bookstore with some danish. "Sorry, I had an errand to do. I thought these might make up for my lateness." He gave her a big smile.

"*You* are the boss, remember? But thanks for the goodies." She poured him a cup of coffee. They sat on the tall chairs in front of the side-counter where they kept the coffee, ate lunch there occasionally, or just chatted about the business. They were barely through their coffee when Paul came up behind them. "I have four books here I would like to take with me today if I may." He placed some money beside the books.

Jackson stood and held out his hand. "Jackson Hunter. You do not have to pay for these books if you plan to return them."

"Great." The man stared at Jackson until the silence became awkward.

Meg spoke, "Mr. Jenkins and his wife are avid readers. They try to guess who the criminal is in their books and see who gets it right. Sounds like fun, right boss?"

Jackson chuckled. "It sure does. Would you like some coffee before you leave?"

"Uh . . . no thank you."

"Where are you from, Mr. Jenkins?"

"Call me Paul. I'm from North Dakota. Are you familiar with that state?"

"Sure. I lived there most of my life. We lived on Raymond Street."

"I thought so."

"What do you mean. Do you know me?"

"Where's your dad and sister living?"

"My dad is in Philadelphia. He has a real estate business. My sister lives here in Cape May. She moved a few years ago."

"You were left in North Dakota alone then."

"No, I traveled throughout the world for quite a while before coming here to open this bookstore."

"I do remember you of course. Everyone in North Dakota remembers your family. I am sorry about your mother. She was a wonderful woman. I hope you didn't blame yourself all these years for her death. You were just a four-year-old little boy."

"What are you talking about?"

Paul Jenkins walked toward the front door. "Do you think we can finish this chat outside?"

Jackson shrugged his shoulders when he turned to Meg before following the gentleman out the door. He led Paul around to the back of the building with a small patio and chairs.

"The only reason I bring this up is to help you understand that you did not kill your mother, as was thought at that time. The local Sheriff will be contacting you shortly. They finally have someone who can testify as to exactly who did kill her." He looked over at Jackson.

He had his head down for a moment. *He was trying to find his voice.*

"You okay, Son?" When Jackson looked up at him, he continued, "Your mother's case has not been touched for almost forty years now. It's important that you are a part of this investigation to clear yourself. You need to grab the opportunity of hearing from the person offering to finally confess they have information. We will be there also. My wife and your mother were close friends. In fact, she was on the phone with your mom when it happened and heard the gunshot. Fortunately, your sister was at our house."

Jackson went numb. He didn't respond right away. Paul waited while trying to console him.

"I had been told by my sister that my mother died of cancer. But then when I turned fifteen, my father told me *I* killed her. I lived with that all these years. How could they have been wrong?"

"Someone planted that gun in your hands and took off after your mother was shot, leaving you to look like you pulled the trigger. Here." Paul handed him a card with a phone number to the Sheriff's office in North Dakota. "Do yourself a favor and call him. I know you will want to clear your name. They need to find the criminal who did this to your family. It's been a cold case long enough."

They walked around the front of the building. Paul leaned into the front door. "Nice meeting you, Meg."

She waved.

"Good luck with your bookstore, and thanks for the coffee, Jackson. Here's my home number. Call any time. I know you took a beating in North Dakota as you got older because people were told you did this. Don't let this go, Son." He patted him on the shoulder and left.

At first, Jackson sat in his car quietly. Meg saw him through the store window. She had just finished cleaning up the place.

When Paul drove his car away, Jackson got out of his car and vomited by the side of the road. He got back into the car and took off with great speed.

Since that was the second car motor Meg heard, she rushed outside just in time to catch Jackson's car turning at the corner. *She couldn't imagine where he would be going. What had Mr. Jenkins told him? She didn't think he would be inconsiderate to take off and leave her there alone when he knew she had children coming in for their program. Who would take care of the customers if they arrived during that hour?*

She wanted to be sure he was okay, so she took a chance and called him.

"Is everything all right? You don't usually run off like this."

"I'm fine. If you get stuck with customers, call me."

"Why don't you come to my house after the children leave today. I'll make you dinner for a change." *She felt terrible, realizing that man gave Jackson some bad news.* "What do you say? I'm a good cook."

"I can't right now. Thanks, Meg." The phone went dead. Her children would be there any moment, so she had to let it go.

As she prepared for the program, *her thoughts went back to hearing the man say something about Jackson's mother's death. She sure hoped that was not what she had really heard.*

"Hello, girls. Come right in and have a seat."

"Where's Mr. Hunter?" one of the little girls asked. Her mother told her that was not her business.

"Mr. Hunter had to leave to pick up more books for the store. He will be gone the rest of the day," Meg told the children. She then started their program.

CHAPTER FORTY-FOUR

Cape May, NJ

Jackson had driven his vehicle straight to a local pub in the area. He ordered one whiskey after another until he finally fell off a stool while trying to leave. The owner of the pub took his wallet off the bar and called a number he had listed.

Meg had just finished up with the children. The last one had been picked up. No customers had come in during that time. She was tidying up the children's section when she got the call, "Hello, Hunter's Bookstore."

"Are you Meg Carson?"

"Yes. How can I help you?"

"It seems you have a friend here at our pub on seventh street. His name is Jackson Hunter. I need you or another person to come and pick him up. He has too much liquor in his system to drive away from here."

"Give me fifteen minutes, please." Meg got off the phone and called Kate and Austin's number. "Is your husband home, Kate?"

"Yes. He is not expected to work today. What's going on?"

"I'm sorry to do this to you, but I need strong hands right now to help me get Jackson out of the pub on seventh street. Any chance he would be able to help me?"

"Of course. We'll be right there."

Meg grabbed her bag, locked up the store and took off to the pub. *She was feeling a bit nauseous and afraid for her friend.*

When she parked her car and ran into the place, she barely recognized Jackson. She could only hope this was a one-time splurge. "My friends are only minutes away. They will help me get him out of here," she told the bartender who had propped him up on a chair by the door. "Thank you for calling."

"I've never seen this guy before, so I had to go into his wallet. It was on the counter." The bartender handed it over to her. "Get home safe." He walked along the bar to wait on other customers.

Kate and Austin rushed to the pub. "Sorry it took us so long to get here."

"No problem. I'm grateful you are willing to help me."

They got Jackson out to her car. Austin and Kate followed them to her house. She didn't feel it was appropriate to take him to his room at the Bed and Breakfast in his condition. They finally reached the front door. "He'll stay here tonight. I have an extra room."

"What drove him to do this?" Austin asked as they got him into Meg's home and laid him on the bed in the guest room.

"I have no idea." Her hands were still trembling. "I've never seen him take a drink, other than a small glass of wine during dinner once. But we haven't known one another long enough for me to judge him."

"Did he seem upset today?" Kate asked.

"I'm not sure. He did seem a little off earlier today. I'm hoping to find out what brought this on once he awakens tomorrow morning."

Kate hugged her. "Get some rest now and give me a call when you have time."

"Thanks so much. Have a good night." She hugged Austin. Trying to calm herself, she poured a glass of wine. *She felt guilty judging Jackson for drinking and here she was with the need to have some wine. But she rarely drank alcohol. She felt so mixed up, hoping she hadn't misjudged him of being a great guy. No one is perfect, but this had to have something to do with Paul Jenkins.*

She walked into the second bedroom to check on him and make sure he had covers. While lifting his head to fluff up the pillows, she noted he had a little prayer book. It must have fallen from his pocket when they got him into the bed. She opened it to find his name under the 'to' section. The 'from' section read: 'To a great guy! I love you so much.' It was signed by 'Allison.'

Jackson had never mentioned that name. Maybe she was an old girlfriend, or could he have been married to her? This was more upsetting. *In the shower, she tried to understand why she felt so taken back with this woman's name in a sacred book. Was she herself having feelings for this guy? He had always been kind, polite, and was attractive to her. That was the Jackson she had met months ago. Now, she wasn't sure who he would turn out to be when he awakened.*

Dressing for bed, she decided to try and put it out of her mind.

CHAPTER FORTY-FIVE

Peddler's Village/Lahaska, PA

Dana was excited to once again return to Peddler's Village with her husband. Last year they made the trip as they did every year and had a wonderful time. In fact, that's when they talked about having a baby and naming her Emily Rose, just like the porcelain doll Dana purchased that day.

As they walked around the village, looking into store windows and stopping to pick up a few things, Nick asked, "Are you hoping to get another porcelain doll this year, Dana?"

When she looked over at him, he had a big grin on his face. He put his arm around her tighter, waiting for an answer.

"That's a joke, right?" She stared into his deep brown eyes she always admired, waiting for a response.

"Just wondering." His dimples active caused her to question that.

"Is that what you want?" She waited while he hesitated a bit.

"Only if you do, Honey. I am good either way."

"That's a great answer, my dear husband, because I think two children and a new grandchild are plenty to keep us busy. Don't you?"

"Oh, yeh, sure. I'm with you. If we have too many children, we might be over-whelmed in finding time for ourselves. Do you think that selfish of me?"

"Absolutely not. I think that is the perfect response since we are not far from turning fifty in a few years." Dana waited for his response.

"Oh no! The dreaded "50." Nick made a face and held his stomach as if he was going to collapse. "Might we check out the store for older couples where they sell canes, walkers and such? We want to be prepared, right?"

Dana smacked his arm with a magazine she had picked up along the trip. "Don't make fun of me. Now let's change the subject and actually do some shopping. And no more books!"

"Well, what do you know! Without being obvious, check out the guy sitting at that outside table alone with a gun handle shining from his belt. Tell me he doesn't look like the sketch the detectives showed us of Brian Walters." Nick put his arm around her and quickly led her past the guy after she glanced over once. "What do you think?"

"I think you may be right. Of course, there are people who resemble others. But, yes, he is a dead ringer for that artist sketch we saw. What should we do?"

"I don't think we should charge after him."

"Why don't we get a little further away, I'll take a photo and you call the detectives."

"Okay, but don't leave my side."

Dana got her very tiny camera from her purse. It was a really good one. She did not need to use a flash with it, so the photo could be taken without anyone realizing they were being photographed. She waited until the suspect looked up from the newspaper he was reading. Then she took the shot. She was in back of some beautiful flowers and was sure he didn't see her. *I don't believe he would know either of us anyway. We never met him before.*

Nick was off the phone in minutes. "Detective Mason wants us to send him the photo right away. I am sending him the location information now. They are going to contact the precinct up here."

Dana did as she was told. When Nick shut his phone down, he reached for her arm. "Let's get out of here just in case he gets suspicious."

"I wonder why he would be hanging out way up in this area. Do you suppose he lives here?"

"Babe, I have no idea. He has to hide somewhere. Let's just move on and get something to eat at our favorite restaurant."

"I thought you wanted to leave now."

"We have to eat. If he is in the restaurant, we will get out of there right away. Aren't you hungry?"

"Yes, but afraid also that he might be in there."

"I'll go in first and look around. If I don't see him, I'll wave to you."

Nick walked through the restaurant, even into the men's bathroom. There was no sign of the sketch he had viewed of Brian Walters.

He went back to his car. "I don't see him anywhere. Let's go."

At the *Cock & Bull* a waiter arrived within minutes. The place was not filled up yet with all who usually dined there.

Dana ordered her favorite, "I'll have the scallop and shrimp linguini, please. Seltzer water with lime is fine."

"I'll have the lobster with baked potato and black coffee."

"We are such creatures of habit, aren't we, Nick?"

"I suppose so. That's a good thing. We are not always doing the same things over-and-over. I think it's only with food and beverages."

"Maybe you are right. Hey, you don't think this guy is following us, do you?" Dana suddenly got the goosebumps all over her arms.

"Why would he? He has no idea who we are in this big mob of people around here this time of year. Plus, he has never met either of us."

Once they were finished their dinner, Dana put a scare into her husband. "Don't forget that this guy followed my brother to our home twice now. You don't think he might have been in the area in Cape May where he saw us come from or go into our home?"

"I suppose that's a possibility. But he has never done anything to us or broken into our house."

"Can we leave now Nick? I'm sorry to break up our enjoyment, but I'm scared. It reminds me too much of Matthew's antics."

"No arguments from me, Honey. We will go now." They left the restaurant, both glancing around them for Walters. He hugged his wife tightly as they walked past the shops to their car.

Dana opened her own door this time and quickly got into the passenger seat. "Do you see him anywhere?"

"I'm not looking, but if you want me to, I will."

"No, just get into the car and let's get out of here." She was trembling in her speech and itching her arms.

As they drove away, Nick looked in his rear-view mirror, but saw no one following them.

******

Detective Mason spoke with the Detectives at the Lahaska precinct after getting off the phone with Nick. He let them know they may have a killer staying in their Peddler's Village area. After giving them a full description of Brian Walters and other pertinent information, the detectives took off for the long ride up to the village to check the place out and leave some posters. It was only two p.m. when they left Philadelphia. They hoped to be able to weed this vicious criminal out if he is at the right location.

Carla was restless in her seat, knowing how long the ride would be. *She had spent some time in Lahaska before. It's a beautiful, entertaining place, but not this time for them.* "What did the detectives have to say?"

"They are getting all their officers out in that area and beyond right now. We are expected to stop in there after we get to look around once we arrive. Have you ever been there before?"

"Plenty of times. How about you, Brock?"

"Never. This will be a first for me. I understand there are a lot of places this guy could hide."

"True. Lots of restaurants, all kinds of shops, amusements, and places to stay, etc. It may not be so easy to find him."

"He could also be back in Philadelphia or New Jersey now." Brock left out a heavy sigh. "But we have to check it out right away in case he is laying low in the village."

"I agree."

They decided to stop at the precinct first to let them know they were there and were anxious to relate how difficult this killer is to catch.

When they arrived, Detective Brett Lopez met them at their car.

CHAPTER FORTY-SIX

Cape May, N.J.

When Meg arrived at the bookstore after the weekend was over, she noted Jackson's car behind the building. They hadn't spoken since he left the bookstore after he and Mr. Jenkin's had a conversation. Jackson left her home in the middle of the night before she could find out what happened that he had to go and get drunk. Kate told her he did not show up at the Bed & Breakfast to sleep either.

Meg entered the store. He was at the counter in the front flipping through a stack of pages in a folder.

"How are you feeling?" Meg put her bag down and looked up at him.

"I am feeling embarrassed that you had to take me to your house drunk. I can think of a million ways to say I'm sorry, but I know that wouldn't be enough."

"It's your business, Jackson. If I'm going to work for you, though, I need to know that this is not a regular thing you do."

"You mean getting drunk?"

"Yes." She poured herself some coffee and sat next to him at the counter.

"I have never done this before. I don't drink, except for a glass of wine occasionally like most people. Look, I don't want to lose you as an employee or as a good friend. It will be difficult, but I think I owe it to you to share why that happened, unless you are okay without hearing it."

"I'm not okay. It hurt me deeply to see you in that condition. I'm thankful this was a one-time thing. If you want to share, fine. But it's not necessary to keep me working here with you. I love being here, and I would never quit."

"Thank you, Meg. You mean a lot to me."

She looked up in surprise and he turned away. "I believe you are the kindest woman I have ever met." He turned toward her. "Mr. Jenkins was here to assure me I did not kill my mother at the age of four. At the age of fifteen my father told me I was the killer."

Meg couldn't believe her ears. She lost her voice for a second. No wonder he acted the way he did last night. This poor man lived with that all these years. "I am so sorry, Jackson."

"Mr. Jenkins and his wife and young daughter lived down the street from us. He remembers the incident well because his wife was on the phone with my mother when the gunshot was heard on Mrs. Jenkins end of the receiver. She called the police. When they got there, Mr. Jenkins told me it was on record that I was sitting on the floor holding the shotgun. No one else was in the house but my dead mother. *Meg had to hold back her tears for him.* My sister was at the Jenkins house with their daughter when it happened." He stopped to take a drink of water. He put his head down for a moment, then continued. "When the police arrived, naturally they thought I pulled the trigger."

"Mr. Jenkins relayed to me that the police department in North Dakota, where we all lived, opened the cold case a few months back. They have been trying to find out where I am living. Jenkins was told they have someone who has a photo of a possible suspect. He's an older man who was afraid at that time to step forward because he feared my dad, as many did in those days I'm told. My father was always a bit of a bully and his size didn't help. People in the area were afraid to cross him in any way. Mr. Jenkins recognized my name and the fact that I lived in North Dakota and put two-and-two together."

He sat silent. Meg reached over and touched his arm. They sat that way for a while before she finally spoke. "I don't know how you lived through all that, Jackson. Are you and your father close?"

"Not at all. He told me that shocking fact when I was fifteen-year's-old. It caused me to believe that I killed my own mother. I never wanted to see him again. I guess I felt it was a mean thing to do. He should have kept it to himself and went looking for my mother's real killer, instead of marrying another woman right away. That's what I would have done if it were my child of four taking the blame."

"It must have been really rough on you to live with them after that."

"Oh, I didn't live with them. I took off on my own and stayed with friends my father never knew about. I worked with a friend and his dad in mechanics, fixing cars, etc. until I was old enough to go out on my own. He never came looking for me. Once I was in my twenties, I got into real estate and made good money for years, traveled some for a while and then ended up here in Cape May. It was my lucky day when I met you."

Meg couldn't help herself. She had to give him a hug. He accepted. They sat for a long time before Jackson stood and reached for her hand. "Enough of my miseries. Let's get out of here. No one has come in today at all. I hope that's not a bad sign. But I have reservations for two for dinner tonight at Viggiano's

Sunset Restaurant in West Cape May to make it up to you, if that's okay."

"You don't have to do that." Meg stood and grabbed her bag from the floor. Jackson took her free arm. "I want to do this, unless you can't go."

"Okay, what time?"

"How's seven-thirty? We can close up at four. Is that enough time for you to get ready?"

"Plenty of time. Are you sure you're up for this tonight?"

"Yes, I actually feel like a huge weight dropped from my shoulders, thanks to you. The least I can do is buy you dinner. I won't take no for an answer." He went to the back of the building to his office. She didn't see him the rest of the day until four p.m. when they closed up the place. He had spent his day in the store office on the phone.

Jackson walked her to the car. "See you soon."

"I'll be ready." *That's the Jackson she knew and loved—oops, as a friend of course.* Going through her clothes, she realized many of her dresses were too large on her now. She decided to run to the mall and select something new. She then rushed home, bathed, dressed, had a glass of wine and looked forward to their dinner.

Meg was impressed with the new restaurant he chose. The lights were low, beautiful music playing in the background, and the service was wonderful. They spent part of the night telling one another funny things that had happened to them in the past. That pushed away her questioning of who Allison was in relationship to Jackson.

"Would you like to dance?"

"Yes. You are the first man I have met over the years who is not afraid to dance."

"Really? Then I might impress you with my ball-room dancing one day."

"Truly? You took ballroom dance lessons?"

"Sure did. I love music, so why not learn to dance to it?"

"How old were you then?"

"About thirty-two I suppose. It's really not so difficult as some think. Come, I will teach you a few steps."

After a luscious dinner and lots of dancing, the couple returned to Meg's house for coffee. They chatted about lighter subjects for a while, like the bookstore, the children, and how Jackson felt Meg needed a raise.

"I'll agree with that. Thank you."

"We'll discuss it tomorrow." He stood, preparing to leave when instead he asked Meg, "Who is this beautiful woman in the photo? She looks a lot like you."

Not prepared for the question, Meg hesitated as her eyes filled with tears.

Jackson turned to face her. "Oh, I am being too nosey."

"It's fine. I'm just sensitive when it comes to my daughter, Laney."

"I noticed you never talk about family."

Meg rose and headed to the bathroom. "Please excuse me a minute."

When she returned, Jackson was pacing the room. "Do you want to share it?"

"I'm fine. I'll see you tomorrow. Thank you for the wonderful dinner. I look forward to my raise also." She forced a smile.

"I won't forget," he promised. "I am on my way to the Bed and Breakfast to apologize to Kate and Austin for my bad behavior. I want them to know that it will never happen again."

"I'm sure they will understand."

After he left, Meg cried her eyes out. She was upset with herself that she couldn't share the pain of having lost her daughter. He was a sensitive man who had lost most of his joy in life thinking he had killed his loved one.

After she calmed down, she looked at the time. It was ten p.m. She wondered if he was still awake. Meg changed her mind three times before she finally called him. "Did I wake you?"

"No. I couldn't sleep. I came outside on the front patio. Austin and Kate retired for the night. Talk to me."

"Would you mind if I came by and sat with you for a bit? I do want to tell you about my daughter if you are willing to listen."

"I will pick you up," Jackson offered.

"That's not necessary. I can drive over. It's only a few blocks. I'll see you soon."

When she ended the call, she almost changed her mind again. *She hoped she wasn't burdening him. He already had his own problems. She wanted so much to help him, not have him worry about her issues. Yet, she wanted him to know she trusted him, since he shared his sorrows.*

Meg quickly locked up the house and drove to the Bed & Breakfast. Once she saw Jackson's face, she knew this was the right thing to do.

He stood up to greet her. Then they sat side-by-side facing one-another on the patio glider.

"It's good you changed your mind about sharing whatever this problem is that you have, Meg. I didn't want to share either. It's embarrassing and I wasn't sure how you would take it . . . me believing I was a killer from a young age."

"I would never judge you, even if it were true. But it's not, so I agree with Mr. Jenkins. You should call Sheriff Joe Speil in North Dakota and get more information. If you don't want to go there alone, I would be able to accompany you since your sister knows how to run the bookstore. Of course, she may want my help here. Don't mind me. I'm just nervous right now. It would make more sense for me to take care of the bookstore and for her to go with you. She is family." Meg hugged herself—a habit she couldn't seem to stop when she felt out of sorts.

Jackson took her hands in his to calm her. "It will be okay . . . all of it. We can talk about you going with me. My sister loves the bookstore and has agreed to run it while I'm gone. Then I will make the call tomorrow to the sheriff in North Dakota and find out exactly what I have to do." He took his hands away. "Now tell me about your daughter."

She took a quick sip of water from a bottle she brought. "Where do I start?" While thinking, she pushed her flaming red hair back off her forehead. "My daughter, Laney, who is married to Charlie . . . Dana and Nick's son, brought my first grandson into the world recently. I will not be allowed to see him. She has disowned me because of a secret I promised my best friend decades ago I would keep forever. I won't go into a lot of detail, but my friend, Grace, became pregnant when we were adults in our twenties, living here in Cape May. She never spoke of the father." She stopped to take a swig of the water again.

"Take your time, Meg. There's no rush."

"Grace got really sick the last three months of her pregnancy. When it was time to deliver her baby, she died in the process."

Jackson handed her a small pack of tissues from his pocket to wipe her silent tears.

"She knew how sick she was and that there was a good chance this could happen. So right before her delivery she begged me to take her child and raise her as my own. She made me promise to never tell anyone, especially Laney, that she was not my biological child." She dabbed her eyes.

"I kept the secret and never did tell my daughter. I raised her from the moment they put her in my arms at the hospital . . . right after Grace died." She put her head down, covering her eyes. "I'm sorry I am so emotional."

"It's not surprising. I hear and feel your pain, Meg. Let it out."

She should never have shared that with him. She bawled while he held on tight to her. After about fifteen minutes, she pulled herself together. "I am sorry. This happens whenever I talk about my daughter. Fortunately, Laney and Glen, the baby, do not have any signs of the illness Grace had when she delivered. They both have to be checked annually to make sure they are not carriers. But I know Laney. She is strong and doesn't concede easily. This was a terrible shock to her. I should not have waited so long. She told me she never wanted to see me again, and I would not see Glen either."

"I suppose you have called her since?"

"She doesn't answer my calls, sends mail back to me unopened, and also sends back any gifts I mail for my grandson. The one highlight is her husband, Charlie. Dana told me the other day that he feels my sorrow so he will be sending me photos of Glen. Dana promised to keep me informed periodically, so I know they are doing well."

"You were brave to tell your daughter the truth. It will be up to her to realize how much she needs you. I am sure that will come one day. In the meantime maybe you could use a vacation while I work things out with my mother's cold case."

She looked into his glassy blue eyes. "I promise to stay out of the way. In fact, I have cousins who live there I can visit with also. My purpose for offering to go, though, is to support you, Jackson."

He put his arm on her shoulder. "Thank you. It means a lot to have someone like you in my corner. Now, what do you say I get you a glass of wine?"

"That's a great idea. Thanks."

She waited outside while Jackson tip-toed into the Bed & Breakfast to get her drink. She felt good that she had shared the hole in her heart with him.

He certainly had one himself. She hoped she would be able to be a good support for him when he deals with the legal system in his hometown.

CHAPTER FORTY-SEVEN

Cape May, N.J.

Jackson received a call in his office.

"Hello, Jackson Hunter?"

"Yes. How can I help you?"

"This is Sheriff Joe Speil in North Dakota. I am contacting you to let you know your mother's case that was re-opened months ago is still active. We have found a strong eyewitness to the crime. I understand you wanted to be contacted as to when you should to be a part of this development. Would it be possible for you to be here by the end of this week?"

"Yes. I will have someone else with me."

"That's fine."

"Since it is quite a distance from New Jersey, we will leave here tomorrow morning."

"Excellent. We will pay for the plane tickets. How many will you need?"

"Two and thank you."

"Good. I look forward to meeting you."

"We'll see you then."

Jackson sat back in a daze for a second. It seemed so strange that he was going back to a place that forced him to leave in order to not be known for killing his mother.

Meg came up behind him since the door was open. "Hey, are you ready for lunch? My kids just left. If you have too much work, we could order out."

"Let's do that. What do you think about leaving for North Dakota tomorrow morning?"

"Uh—okay. Are they ready for you?"

"Only if you feel tomorrow is not a rush."

"If they want you now, we are going. You need to get this behind you. Just give me a time and I'll be ready." She put her hand on his shoulder. "I'll put our order in, then we can discuss what they told you if you'd like. A hoagie or what?"

"That's fine. Don't forget your Cole Slaw," he teased.

The bookstore was empty of customers. She set up their lunch on the front counter when it all arrived. Jackson returned from getting them milkshakes just as the hoagies were delivered.

"Thanks for setting things up. There was a long line at the ice-cream shop today."

"No problem. I'm famished though. I tried to wait for you but had to get at least one bite into my stomach."

He laughed as he opened his hoagie. "Not much belly there, so you'd better fill it."

"Checking out my belly, eh? That's odd."

"Well, not really. When men see a good figure, it's just natural they check it out."

"By men, you include yourself, right?"

"Sure, why not? I'm not married."

"Were you ever married, Jackson?"

She noted he didn't answer right away and, in fact, took a bite of his hoagie first.

"Sorry, that was rude. I shouldn't be so nosy."

"No need to apologize. I have never been married, but once engaged for a short time. I broke it off when I discovered she was cheating on me. That's not the kind of marriage I visualized for my future."

"Sorry to hear that. At least you found out before you married her."

"Yes, a stroke of luck there."

While discussing their trip, they finished lunch. She cleaned everything up while Jackson took a phone call in the office.

When he returned, he tapped her on the shoulder. She had been cleaning off the counter.

"I'm thinking of closing the shop for the rest of the day, unless you have something scheduled."

"Not a thing. But why?"

"As you know, we will be leaving early in the morning for our trip. Relaxing for a while, having dinner out later, and to bed early would be a good idea. What do you think?"

"I agree. I still have to pack."

"Would you mind if my sister and her fiancé joined us for dinner? I thought it might be a good opportunity for you to get to know one another."

"I look forward to that, Jackson. What a great idea. What time is dinner?"

"If I pick you up at seven tonight will that be enough time for you to rest and pack?"

"It's perfect. Let's get out of here."

He locked up. They waved goodbye and each drove away in their own cars.

When Meg arrived home, she parked her car and went into the house. The first thing she did was her 'happy dance.' *It was the first time in months of depression and sorrow, that she felt her life had returned again.*

CHAPTER FORTY-EIGHT

Cape May, NJ

J ackson arrived at Meg's home right on time. It was a short distance to the restaurant.

"Wow! Don't take this the wrong way, but you sure clean up good."

"Since I think that was meant as a compliment, I will accept it as one." *He always made her feel good. It was the first time she wore a sexy dress in years. She had rushed to a shop to purchase it as soon as they had left the bookstore earlier.*

"I have to say that you always look handsome, my friend. I notice women checking you out all the time, even when they come into the bookstore with their children."

Jackson's mouth formed the letter O. "Really? Thanks for telling me. I never noticed."

She giggled. "Right."

When they arrived at the *Sapore Italiano* in West Cape May, well known for their Italian fare, Jackson gave his keys to the man who held the door open for Meg. Then he took her arm and led her into the beautiful room where they would have dinner.

"Hey, Sis. You beat us here."

"We actually arrived only a few minutes ago. Good choice, Brother. I have never been here before."

"Neither have I. Allow me to introduce you ladies. This lovely woman next to me is Meg Carson. She is a friend and also the one who helps me run the bookstore."

"Nice to meet you, Meg." His sister shook her hand across the table.

"This is my sister Allison." It was Meg's turn to be surprised. *She never guessed that heartwarming letter to Jackson she had come upon recently was signed by his sister.*

"It's really a pleasure to meet you, Allison."

"We left the best for last," Jackson chuckled. "This amazingly good-looking man is my sister's fiancé, Roberto Diaz."

"Oh, future brother-in-law, you make me blush. Although I do agree with your description of me." It was his turn to tease.

The waiter came to their table. "The first order should be Champagne. We are celebrating being together," Jackson looked over at Meg. She smiled.

"Are we all ready to order our dinner?"

"We are," his sister offered.

"How about you, Meg?"

"I know what I'd like for dinner."

Jackson turned to her. "You go first then." Meg ordered a Salmon platter with Cole Slaw, as usual, and a baked potato.

Allison and Roberto chose spaghetti and meatballs that turned out to be the size of golf balls.

"You could make them at home," Jackson told his sister.

"Not to taste as good as what an Italian Restaurant serves."

"That's true. I'll have the London Broil, baked potato, and the Baklava."

"I know you are picking up the tab on this order," his sister teased him.

Meg questioned his order. "What is it made from? I've never heard of Baklava."

"It's a pastry with nuts, sugars, butter and some spices."

"Not something I would eat, but you enjoy it, Brother." Allison never had the same taste buds as her brother.

"I shall. Now, let's talk about our trip and you, my dear sister, taking over the bookstore. I know you are familiar with everything in it. But if you have questions, ask them now." He poured the Champagne while she spoke.

"I'm good. I've been in there enough times that I know where everything is located. You remember, I hope, that I helped you set up the place way before the opening. I will also continue with the children's programs Meg set up. If I have a question, I can always call you. Now, tell us how you two met."

"First, let's make a toast."

"I would like to make it," Allison offered.

"Go ahead."

"I'd like to make a toast to our new friend, Meg, and to my brother, Jackson. We wish you both a safe trip and a good outcome in North Dakota."

They clinked glasses. "That was very kind of you, Sis."

After dinner, over coffee they chatted about themselves so they could get to know one another better. Allison told some funny stories about her brother, causing Meg's cheeks to sting from laughing so much. She really took a liking to Jackson's sister. Then her fiancé had some fun things he shared with them, like how many times Allison checks everything before bed.

"I believe that's called OCD. She has had the problem for years now." "Okay guys knock it off. Let's change the subject, shall we?" Allison covered her eyes with her hands for a moment. "Tell us, Meg. Do you have any children?"

She hesitated for a moment, not sure how to answer that question, but finally decided to just say, "Yes, I have a lovely daughter, Laney, a wonderful son-in-law, Charlie, and a newly born grandson, Glen." *She didn't know how she got through all that with a smile, but she was determined not to wreck the evening.*

Jackson quickly cut in, "We had better get going now. We have an early morning call to leave for North Dakota. Let's go people. I got this." He handed cash to the waiter.

Before they got into their cars, they hugged outside the restaurant and promised to keep in touch.

Meg turned to Jackson. "It was a great evening. Thanks so much for including me."

"You'll be part of the family in no time." Alison smiled at her.

Meg wasn't sure what she meant by that. Could she be referring to the two of them being much more than friends?

They arrived back at Meg's little house on the river. "This evening was enjoyable. I wouldn't have planned it without you, Meg. Get some sleep. I'll pick you up at eight a.m. We have a long trip tomorrow so dress comfortably. I'll bring the drinks and other goodies."

"You are too much." She waved as he drove away.

CHAPTER-FORTY-NINE

Cape May, NJ

M eg had little sleep. She was too excited about what lay ahead for them in North Dakota. She showered, dressed, and had some coffee by the time her doorbell rang.

It was Jackson. He picked her up right on time, brought out her one large suitcase and a smaller one, along with a heavy warm coat. They expected it to be fairly cold there in October and hope to be back in Cape May before November's weather hits.

With his big smile, Jackson asked, "Did you get some sleep?"

"Not much, but I'm okay. I am too excited to sleep." She chuckled.

Once in the car, he suggested they make a quick stop at their favorite café for breakfast before getting on the road. "What do you think?"

"Great idea since I skipped eating because of the time."

"Same here."

They only spent about forty-five minutes in the café, anxious to get on the road. Both had eggs and sausage. They took more coffee with them.

Before Jackson opened Meg's door on the passenger side of his car, he asked her, "Are you sure you want to go through this with me? I'll understand if you want to back out now, Meg."

"I will be there every step of the way, just like you have been for me. I know you are my boss at the bookstore, but you are also my friend, remember?"

"I do. Thank you."

When they closed the trunk and she got into the van, Meg turned to him. "It seems like we both suffered for years. I finally released my worries. Let's get going so you can do the same."

For a second, he looked over at her with a grin. Then he started the engine and took off for the airport.

CHAPTER-FIFTY

The Jersey Shore

The Pearson's are finally able to pick up their son at the drug rehabilitation center at the Jersey Shore. Ben did his six months and it sounds to Michael he has done well. *Ben's reaction to all of the changes in their lives that would affect his son terrified Michael. He wanted Jessica to be a part of this also, so she wouldn't scare Ben right up front. He had no choice but to introduce her to his other family. He chose to do it when they met up with her at Roger's home where she now lived.*

As Jessica came out of the house, Michael, Nicky, Michaela, and Becky walked over to her.

"Hi, Mom." Becky gave her a kiss on the cheek. "How are you feeling?"

"I'm fine and excited to finally bring Ben home." She glanced over at Nicky and Michaela.

"Jessica, I would like you to finally meet Nicky Collins, my fiancé, and our daughter, Michaela Pearson."

After a long stare, she politely accepted them. "It's nice to meet you both."

Michael felt that Jessica knew she caused their marriage to fail and was now living with her long-time lover. What else could she say? He almost wanted to laugh out loud but supressed the feeling.

"Okay, let's discuss how we are going to bring Ben into all the changes that have been made. It will affect his life too. We should do it without it causing him too much drama." Becky was happy to speak up for the safety of her brother.

"Mom, the police are still trying to find out who this criminal is who has been stalking dad. He almost killed you both. Because of that, we feel that as much as we would like to introduce Ben to Nicky and Michaela, and also have him live with us, it would be too much for him right now. So, we suggest you take him to live with you and Roger until the detectives find dad's stalker."

"That's wonderful. I am sure Roger will love having Ben with us."

"Good." Michael put his head down for a moment to compose himself. *The last thing he wanted to do was to leave his son in Roger's home, but knew they had no other choice for him to be safe. Any contact with Michael could cost his son's life.* "Becky and I would appreciate some time alone with Ben at the rehabilitation center, or on the grounds once he is released before he leaves with you."

"I have no problem with that. It's a lovely day. Maybe after he checks out you could be alone with him on the grounds outside where they have benches set up under the trees."

"Thank you, Jessica." *He was shocked that she was so compliant.*

Nicky looked over at Michael. "We should be on our way now. It was nice to meet you, Jessica."

"Oh, same here." Jessica's face lit up. "You are not going with us?"

Michaela smiled at her and turned toward their car.

Michael spoke up, "They only came along so you could meet one another. Now they are driving to a friend's place not far from our home. Becky and I will stop there before we all go home later. Our detectives want us to stay together to be safe."

"I wondered why a police car with two officers followed you here."

"They are not only following to keep us safe. Detectives Mason and Hall want them to also sign Ben out from the rehabilitation center. As you know, he was signed in by their officers when he first came to the center."

"I see. Well, I'm ready to leave."

Becky looked over at her mom. "Why don't you ride with me and dad? It will be easier taking one car. We can drop you and Ben off here on our way back."

"Sure, we can do that." She stepped into the back seat of Michael's car.

It blew Michael's mind that Jessica agreed.

He turned to Nicky and Michaela, giving them both a hug. "Drive carefully please. That culprit doesn't know your car, so you should be okay until you get to your friend's home. Promise to call me as soon as you get there."

"I promise. Enjoy your time with your son." Nicky and Michaela got into her car and took off in the opposite direction.

CHAPTER FIFTY-ONE

Bucks County, PA

Later, Jessica gave her ex-husband a call. "Michael, it appears our son is very interested in meeting your fiancé and daughter."

"How did you make that happen?"

"After talking with Ben, I realized how different he is since his time at the rehabilitation center. So, I took the chance of telling him about Nicky and Michaela, and how you want them to meet him."

"He's okay with that?" Michael's mouth fell open as she spoke.

"At first, he was shocked, especially when I told him we were divorced now. He asked how I felt about that. I told him we both feel we will all have a better life this way. I explained to him how Becky told you that for a long time we both suffered because we were not happy together. But we didn't want to hurt either of our children."

"How did he take that news?"

"He became quiet for a bit, then asked when he could meet Nicky and Michaela. I told him I would call you and see how soon we could visit."

"Right now!" Michael couldn't believe this was happening.

"Okay. We can leave here in about an hour."

"Thanks so much, Jessica. I am grateful you are willing to do this."

"No problem. See you all soon." With that she broke the connection.

Michael turned and hugged his girls. "Smack me somewhere once so I know this is not a dream." With all smiles, they poked him in the belly instead having heard the conversation with Jessica.

"Let's finish breakfast so we are ready for them when they arrive. I am glad the pool is heated in case Ben would like to hang out there while he's here," Nicky commented.

They finished eating, cleaned everything up, then while Michael took a shower and dressed, Michaela set the table in the dining room with pretty plates, cups, saucers, and utensils. She knew Nicky had made a cake earlier and she and Becky had gone out to pick up some donuts.

"I am excited to have a brother." Michaela danced around the room once again. "I feel like the luckiest girl in the world. It's lonely being the only child in the family. Having two siblings will be so much fun."

Becky took her hand. "Dear sister, you are no longer alone, and we will always love you." When they hugged, it brought tears to Michael's eyes. He couldn't fully imagine how much his children had suffered until now.

"Cheer up." Becky hugged her dad. "The past is gone. We are all going to live in the present now. Let's enjoy it together."

Michael hugged her back. "You always know the right things to say, Becky." They all heard the doorbell.

Michael felt his heart flutter a few times. He could also feel his face flush, and he had to pocket his hands from shaking.

Becky looked at her dad. "I'll get it," she offered.

"Hi Ben!" She hugged her brother, then her mom. "Thanks for coming."

"Hi Dad." Ben put his hand out. Michael took it and put it around him as he hugged his son tightly. "I am so happy to see you here, Son. Come, have a seat in the dining room while I introduce you to my fiancé, Nicky, and our daughter, your sister, Michaela."

Ben hesitated, then walked over and shook both their hands. "Hi, nice to meet you."

"Let me take your coats." Michaela took them to the coat rack nearby.

"Let's get comfortable." Nicky led them to the dining room table where Michaela had put out all the goodies, along with cold drinks and coffee.

"Dig in," Michael told his son. "These are the best donuts around."

Ben chuckled and took one. "What grade are you in at school, Michaela," he asked while sitting next to her at the table.

"I'm going into seventh grade this year. How about you?"

"I've missed a lot of school because of my poor behavior. But that has changed. I have one more year before I graduate and don't intend to wreck it this time."

"That's wonderful." Becky patted her brother on the back. "I am proud of you Ben."

"We all are," Michael assured him. "It's amazing how much that center has changed you."

"I'm excited that Roger offered to get me into a part-time school program twice a week to learn carpentry so I can make a living. Those two days I will leave my high-school classes early to study at the carpentry program school. By the time I finish this last year, I will be able to learn more about carpentry at Roger's business."

"I'm happy for you." Becky's beautiful smile revealed how much her brother meant to her.

Nicky and Michaela both wished him all the best with his future career, and Michael gave him a high-five. "You are going places, my boy."

By this time, they had all finished at the table. Nicky stood. "We can clean this up later. How about a tour of our grounds? We have a heated swimming pool if you would like to try it out, Ben."

"I'll put my suit on and swim with you." Michaela offered. "How about you Becky?"

"I'll join you both. What do you think mom? Do you want to swim?"

"I think I'll pass on that. But I would love to see the grounds."

"We also have a screened in patio in the back."

"While you show them the grounds, I will put a roast in the oven." Nicky went into the kitchen.

"Wow, dad, this place is awesome!" It was the most excited Michael had seen his son in a few years.

"I am glad you agreed to come here today, Ben. I hope you realize that our home will always be your home too."

Nicky came out with a large pot of coffee and some mugs, along with a crate of cold drinks for those who did not drink coffee.

Michael, Nicky and Jessica were now sitting in the screened in patio with their coffee. The kids returned from exploring the grounds more.

"Why don't you all put your suits on and dive into the pool," Michael suggested. "I have a swimsuit of mine you can keep, Ben."

"Okay dad, sounds good." He followed Michael and the girls into the house. When they reached the master bedroom, Michael threw the suit to Ben who was studying the large room.

Michael laughed. "Yes, we like it too." He ruffled his son's hair. "Go change. I'll wait downstairs for you."

Once on the first floor again, he grabbed the donuts to take outside with them. By then Ben came down in his dad's swimsuit. "It's a perfect fit."

"You are welcome to keep it. I have others."

"Thanks."

"Let's get outside so you can have some fun while you are here." Ben joined the girls in the pool.

"I brought more coffee, ladies."

By the time they sat down to dinner, it was six o'clock.

After dinner, they returned to the patio to toast marshmallows. The weather was a bit cool, but the moon was bright.

Around eight p.m., Jessica stood up. "I think we had better get going now. Thank you for making me feel comfortable, Nicky. I can see why Michael loves you so much."

Michael was shocked at Jessica's comment.

"I can't wait to come back and visit again," Ben said.

"Pick a weekend when Josh can drive you up here to spend a few days hanging out at the pool with us," Michael suggested.

Nicky put her arm on Ben's shoulder. "I agree with your dad."

"Thanks guys. I'll do that." Ben hugged his sisters and his dad, and they left for Philadelphia.

"I believe today is the best day of my life--other than when I met you, Honey." Michael quickly added.

CHAPTER FIFTY-TWO

Philadelphia, PA

As her dad had suggested, Becky decided to stay with her family until Britt's murderer is found. They all scheduled their time around one another. No one returns to their home in Bucks County alone at night. Michael did let his guard down some because no black cars had been following him lately. He went to the funeral home to work almost every day now and returns home unscathed.

It was a lovely day. The skies clear and the weather perfect. Michael suggested he take his family to breakfast at a new place before heading to work in Philadelphia.

When they arrived at the restaurant, he pulled a chair over for Nicky.

"Thank you, Michael. I love this place." Their daughters had already chosen their seats.

"What are we having this morning, Ladies?" the waiter sat a basket of warm rolls on the table. "Are you ready to order?" he turned to Michaela.

She spoke up right away. "I'll have a spinach omelet with toasted rye bread and a glass of orange juice."

Nicky went next, "I'll have eggs over light with sausage, and coffee."

Becky jumped ahead of her dad, "I'm in the mood for pancakes with some blueberry jam and coffee."

Michael looked over at Becky. "I will have the same. But make sure I have more jam than her."

The young man snickered and left to put in their orders.

Michael studied their young daughter, "Since when do you eat spinach, my dear?"

"I always eat healthy, Dad. You have not been around a lot to notice that. You might be shocked about a lot of growing up I have done recently."

He smiled. "Good. You take after your mother, which is a good thing."

"Yes," Michaela gave her mom a big smile. "I want to be just like you."

Nicky put her coffee down. "Well, I hope that means you will be going to college, as promised. Education is important if you want to get anywhere in this world today."

The waiter brought their breakfast trays. While they ate, they talked about taking a vacation—just the five of them, to a place that was relaxing and enjoyable. After discussing some ideas of where Michael suggested they go, he picked up the tab. "We'll finish this discussion tonight. We have to get to work and you, my sweetheart, have school."

Once they left the restaurant, Michael drove them to their locations and continued to his business in Philadelphia. He also dropped Becky off a few blocks from their funeral home. She had a nail appointment but had to be back in time for her client in an hour. "Enjoy the relaxation, Becky," he yelled to her. She threw him a kiss.

When he arrived at their business, he knew he would be there for most of the day, so he parked in his garage across from the funeral home. *He felt lucky the criminal the police were still looking for had not been on the road since the incident in Cape May.*

As he waited for his client in their main office, he thought back to both of the criminal's victims and how odd it was they wore the same color and style shoes during their attack. Then he tried hard to remember exactly what the brutal beast told him over the phone that day as he prepared to kill Jessica Pearson at their funeral home apartment. After going over everything the lunatic relayed to them, it was like a drill in his brain, reaching through his lobes--finally releasing the killer/stalker in his life. In his mind, it was definitely Brian Walters, not only as a murderer, but as his road stalker.

Michael grabbed the phone to contact the Philadelphia detectives to give them his stalker's name—the nerves in his body dancing. He held one hand to his sweaty forehead. Waiting for a response, he heard his outer office door close. Looking up, he stood facing his client. It took all the strength he held in his mind to turn his phone off and greet the gentleman.

He stood and offered his hand, "Michael Pearson."

"You can call me Adam."

"Okay, Adam, have a seat so we can go over your arrangements. I believe you told me over the phone that you want to be buried next to your mother and father."

"That's correct."

"Would you like to select a casket today while you are here?"

"Yes, I would."

"Then you will first need to fill out the paperwork." Michael placed the papers on his desk. He pulled out his chair for Adam. "We'll need a last name as well." *Michael wasn't sure why he kept staring at his client. He did think it strange that the guy had on a cap that almost covered his eyes completely. In addition, he wore very dark sunglasses. His voice was deep. He seemed friendly enough, but something about him bothered Michael.*

When his client was finished the paperwork, they walked down the hall with all the caskets showing. The middle-aged male with boyish features selected a casket right away. "This one will be fine."

"Let me show you the inside," Michael offered. He lifted the heavy lid. After he and his client discussed the type of casket it was, the Adam stated it was just what he wanted. Thus, Michael leaned forward to close the lid and suddenly felt extreme pain in his head. He passed out onto the floor.

His client had knocked him out. Next, he put duct tape on Michael's mouth and tied his arms and legs before hoisting him into the casket. He closed the lid and waited, pacing up and down. When Michael finally started kicking from inside the box, his attacker opened the lid.

"I suppose you thought I had given up destroying your life like you did to me and my loved ones. You messed with the wrong guy when you killed my mother. I want you to feel the agony, pain, and torture you caused my family."

Alert now, Michael could only make noises that made no sense due to the tape on his mouth. He was terrified he would die in the casket if his daughter didn't return to their office soon.

"Remember that sweet old lady who saved your sister, Dana? Yep, I'm her son!"

He kept pacing while he spoke, with his voice rising. "I hope it was worth it to you! As I put this lid down again, you have only forty-five minutes before you stop breathing in there. Sleep tight!" He dropped the lid on the casket. Then he dropped red shoes to the floor that were sealed in a see-through plastic bag. He made sure he left no prints by wearing gloves. Then he took off, rushing to his car in the parking lot outside. He tore out of the area.

******

While Michael was struggling to get out of the casket, his daughter, Becky had just pulled onto their property, passing another car speeding out of their lot. *"I hope that wasn't my client who isn't due for another ten minutes."*

Becky parked her car, grabbed her briefcase and jacket and rushed into the funeral home office, immediately turning on the very loud air-conditioner. Even with the noise, she was grateful the AC worked at all. She dropped everything onto the desk. *Where is that file I brought from home the other day?*

After quickly looking for the client's file in one of their cabinets in the

front office, she figured she must have left it in their apartment next door. Closing the office door behind her, she had not heard her father banging inside the casket a long hall distance from the front office. The racket the old air-conditioner caused drowned out any other sounds.

She ran over to their apartment next to the funeral home to look for the folder. "Here it is," she cheered aloud as she picked it up from her desk in her bedroom. She was ready to return to the office when her phone buzzed.

"Hello, Pearson's Funeral Home. This is Becky Pearson."

The voice on the other end of the call was deep. "Adam here. I must cancel our appointment. I'll call next week."

"Okay, we'll talk to you then." Becky broke the connection and put her phone in her pocket. "At least I can stop rushing now," she mumbled as she tossed the file onto a table nearby, pushed her shoes off, and poured herself a cup of coffee . . .

"A Criminal Always Returns to the
Scene of the Crime."

JUDY ADAMS JONES

Stranger DNA's Fine Artist is a retired Registered Nurse,
Wife, Mother, Sister, and Grandmother.
Judy comes from a large family of creative people.
Yet, she never realized her own amazing Artistic Abilities
until she had the time to pick up a brush and canvas.
The scene in the middle of the Book Cover is her Stunning Work.

JOE SAVIN

Stranger DNA's Graphic Designer is also a Filmmaker,
Freelance Videographer and Educator.
Joe teaches Journalism and Video Production in several schools.
He spends his free time making short films, playing music,
and exploring the great outdoors with his cat, Genie.

AUTHOR'S COMMENTS

Thank you for Reading
Stranger DNA—Mason *& Hall Series*
Book Two
*

Honest Reviews left on Amazon
are used for helping others
select books based on the
opinions of fellow readers.
*

Thank you!

Amazon.com/stranger-dna-mason-hall-
book/dp/0578923416

www.ingramcontent.com/pod-product-compliance
Lightning Source LLC
Chambersburg PA
CBHW030154200626
46812CB00017B/1918